Title: Wolves at the Door

Author: Steve Watkins

On-Sale Date: December 3, 2024

Format: Jacketed Hardcover

ISBN: 978-1-5461-0998-3 || Price: $18.99 US

Ages: 8–12

Grades: 3–7

LOC Number: Available

Length: 288 pages

Trim: 5-1/2 x 8-1/4 inches

Classification: War & Military; Action & Adventure /
Survival Stories; People & Places / Europe; Social Themes /
Emigration & Immigration

---------------- *Additional Formats Available* --------------
Ebook ISBN: 978-1-5461-0999-0

Scholastic Press
An Imprint of Scholastic Inc.
557 Broadway, New York, NY 10012
For information, contact us at:
tradepublicity@scholastic.com

WOLVES
AT THE
DOOR

WOLVES AT THE DOOR

THE DOOR

STEVE WATKINS

SCHOLASTIC PRESS / NEW YORK

Library of Congress Cataloging-in-Publication Data available

ISBN 978-1-5461-0998-3

10 9 8 7 6 5 4 3 2 1   24 25 26 27 28

Printed in the U.S.A.   128

First edition, December 2024

Book design by Stephanie Yang

FOR EVAN AND JACOB

Map TK

Map TK

CHAPTER 1
ASTA

We are in the shelter near our apartment building in Königsberg when the bombing starts, the swelter of August trapped underground with us. The explosions are distant, east of the city. We feel slight tremors, but the walls only shake a little. The British planes must have missed most of their targets. As soon as the bombing ends, everyone floods out of the shelter for air. Almost everyone. I am halfway up the narrow stairway when Mama calls me back. "Asta! Asta!" I want to ignore her, to keep going, to drink in the fresh air, but my younger sister, Pieta, is too frightened and refuses to leave.

We are still in the shelter two nights later when the bombers return. Pieta's fear is what saves us. Now few of the others make it underground in time. Even from the shelter, deep below the city center, we can feel the full shock of the detonations and the terrible heat from the fires above.

When we emerge, there are bodies in the streets. Broken bodies. Burned bodies. Barely recognizable bodies. I cover Pieta's eyes as we pick our way through the rubble, carrying what little food and clothes we packed for the shelter, and we follow Mama like tightrope walkers across the remains of the last standing bridge over the Pregel River. I keep my own eyes averted as much as I can, but I still see so much loss and pain. I am afraid to look too closely—afraid I will see the faces of my friends. Our neighbors. My teachers. There are more bodies in the water. People dying all around us. We see a small child standing in the road with almost no clothes left on. Mama picks him up and carries him with us for a long time. Then she stops and lays him on the side of the road, where he is still and quiet. Mama takes our hands and pulls us away, farther from the city, crying quietly as we move on.

A week later, we are a hundred sixty kilometers from Königsberg. Mama says we are safe here on our grandparents' farm at the edge of the Romincka Forest, not far from the Polish border. It is where she grew up, before she married Papa and moved to the city. Pieta and I share a bed in the airless attic. When I close my eyes, I see it all again—the terrible aftermath of the bombing—so I make myself stay awake at night for as long as I can.

CHAPTER 2
PIETA

There. Now I have named all the ducks on Opa and Oma's farm, and I can tell them apart, too. *Good morning, Karin,* I say. *Good afternoon, Renate.* So what if I have taken the names from the boys and girls at my school? Karin, Renate, and also Monika, Ursula, Hans, and Peter, and Klaus, and Wolfgang . . .

Maybe there is still a school. Maybe there is not still a school. I don't want to ask Mama. I don't want to know. Maybe there is still a Karin, a Renate, a Monika Ursula Hans Peter Klaus Wolfgang. Maybe there is not. It is also something I don't want to know.

Sometimes I pretend we are still there: on the playground, on the marching grounds, in the classroom doing our sums, in reading circle. One day to trick our teacher, Frau Rust, we girls all changed our hair to the same braided halo style so we looked identical, and we sat in one another's seats in our matching school uniforms to confuse her. I was shy about doing it, but the other girls made me. "It won't work without you, too, Pieta," they said, and I secretly liked that I was included. Usually I watched them from a distance, how they acted, and I rehearsed when I was alone so I could be like them, too. Frau Rust informed Headmistress Bloch. Headmistress Bloch informed all the parents and the grandparents. Many had been orphaned by the war. Many had only their mamas, like Asta and me, because their papas are in the army and away. I don't even remember our papa, or only a little. Only from a long time ago.

Frau Rust smiled when Headmistress Bloch came with a riding crop and ordered all the girls to stand in line with our hands out in front of us, palms up. And down the line she went, *crack, crack, crack.* I can still feel it on my palms, even now at Opa and Oma's farm, but I didn't complain about it to Mama. I don't complain about anything here, either. I try not to speak at all. Since Königsberg, it is best not to speak. Only whisper. If you speak too loudly, your own voice echoes in the bomb shelter and comes back to you and gives you a headache from the screaming that you don't even realize at first is you. Then you tell yourself you must stop screaming but you can't, not as long as the bombs are outside dropping on the city, on everyone not in the shelter. So few were left in the shelter. They thought it was safe to return to their homes, but they were wrong.

CHAPTER 3
ASTA

The young Wehrmacht guards are supposed to be watching the prisoners on my grandparents' farm—the Allied soldiers from France and England and Scotland sent to East Prussia to work after all the paid laborers were drafted into the army. Mostly the guards just sit around and play cards, or eat, or take naps in the barn, their guns left unattended in the horse stalls. Opa and Oma don't mind and never say anything. They treat everyone like family, anyway, guards and prisoners alike. Opa says the prisoners are good workers all on their own. But really, where would they go if they ever tried to escape? North, beyond Königsberg, is the Baltic Sea. East and south is Lithuania. West is Poland. They are a long way from home.

But Opa predicts all this will change soon. Not just because of the bombing of Königsberg, but also because the German army is being forced to retreat from all over—from France in the west and from the Soviet states in the east. And the Soviets are getting closer to East Prussia every day. Opa tells us the Soviets have vowed to drive the entire German population out of East Prussia, but Hitler has ordered the Wehrmacht to shoot anyone who tries to flee, anyone who won't stand and fight. It's hard to believe that these young guards would ever do such a thing as that. Most of the grown men have been gone for years, drafted like Papa into the army long ago. Until the bombing, Mama made monthly trips across Königsberg to the military records office to see if there was word of him because we had long since stopped getting letters.

"The eastern front" was all they would say. "Still on the eastern front."

Now just these young guards—these boys—are all the army that's left, at least here. One of them, Rolf, who is only seventeen, spent most of one day carving a toy wagon for Pieta, with wheels that turn, and now he's carving a horse to go with it. Pieta lost all her toys in the bombing. I lost all my books and dolls, but so far no one has offered to make me any new ones. No new clothes, either, to replace everything else that was left behind and destroyed. Now I mostly wear Mama's old sack dresses and wool leggings and work boots from when she was a girl growing up on Oma and Opa's farm.

Opa listens to the radio at night. Not just the official Nazi Party channels, but the other ones, too—forbidden broadcasts from secret locations in Poland. Sometimes the guards even listen with him.

The prisoners are locked in their cottages by then. Opa, who knows Polish, translates for the guards. Mama insists that Pieta and I leave the room when they do this, even though she herself stays. I overhear some things anyway. One night I hear Opa say that the Red Army has now crossed into Poland. He says the Polish Home Army and the Polish Resistance fighters have even attacked our German army in the streets of Warsaw.

All day, whenever I'm not looking after Pieta, I watch the road for signs of the Red Army invading us next. I listen for the sounds of troops and tanks. I stare at the sky, fearful of more planes and more bombs.

CHAPTER 4
PIETA

Asta says why don't we visit the pigs, but I only want to play with the ducks. I like the pigs, too, but I know what Opa does to the pigs. I've seen them, *after*, hanging in the smokehouse. When the hounds are lapping up black blood from the ground. That's why I don't care for the hounds. They're only doing what they have the instinct to do. I know about animals and their instincts from school. But I don't like it, what the hounds do. The same as the foxes. The same as everything. Maybe the same as people, but I don't always understand their instincts. Maybe people don't have instincts. Maybe we are the only animal that doesn't. Maybe we're not animals at all. But what are we, then?

At school, Frau Rust said the Jews are animals, but Mama said Frau Rust is wrong, that Jews are just people, too, like everyone else. Down the avenue from our apartment building was a Jewish family, with Jewish children. I wouldn't have known this, but Asta told me. They didn't go to our school. Asta said they used to go to school. One of them, a dark-haired girl, had been in Asta's class. But now they weren't allowed. They weren't allowed in the park where we played, either. They stood outside the fence, across the street, and watched, the dark-haired girl and her little brother. The girl might have waved at Asta, a little wave no one was supposed to see. Asta might have waved back in the same way.

They didn't look like animals to me. Just lonely and sad.

CHAPTER 5
ASTA

By fall, the invasion has begun. Tanks and trucks and artillery and wagons and horses and Wehrmacht soldiers are suddenly everywhere on the farm. The prisoners are ordered to stop their work in the fields and dig trenches next to the road. The Red Army has taken the town of Gumbinnen. They have taken over the power station. They have taken over everything and driven out our soldiers. I am angry at Mama for lying to us, for telling us that the war is a long way off and that we would be safe here on Opa and Oma's farm.

The soldiers talk openly with one another and with Opa. They say they were outnumbered and were forced to retreat, but that reinforcements are coming from Königsberg so they can retake the power station. The soldiers say the Red Army has committed atrocities on the German people in Gumbinnen and the other nearby villages. I have to ask Mama what does it mean, *atrocities*? She only shakes her head. It is Oma who tells me: "It means 'terrible things.'"

Opa shakes his head, too. He says, "They are paying back what the German army has done to their people."

"Our army?" I ask him. Is Opa saying the Wehrmacht has also committed atrocities? But how can that be? Papa—*our* papa— serves in the Wehrmacht.

"Hitler's army," Opa says with disgust. "Not ours."

On the third day the soldiers are here, Mama announces at breakfast that she is taking Pieta and me to gather mushrooms in the Romincka Forest. Opa gives Mama a funny look. "You are going where I think?" he asks, lowering his voice.

Oma busies herself clearing dishes. "Is not a good idea," she huffs. "But I'll say no more."

Past Opa and Oma's fields there are rows of pines. Past the pines there is a fence I've never seen before, and beyond it, a real forest, dark like in a fairy tale. Pieta stops suddenly, perhaps frightened, though I can't see her face to read her expression, and as usual she doesn't say anything. But Mama knows. "It's all right, Pieta," she says. "There are some places where it's safer in the dark. And I'm going to show you one. A place I used to go to when I was your age. A place I would take my friends from school when they visited the farm. A secret place."

I don't know how Mama knows her way so well, or how she knows so much about the Romincka Forest, a hunting preserve once owned by the Kaiser, and now for high Nazi officials only. Opa warned us when we first came to the farm never to wander off here, that armed guards have been known to shoot trespassers. We're nearly running to keep up with Mama, but she won't slow down, and when the forest opens onto a meadow—Mama calls it a heath—she tells us we must race across the field as quickly as we can. Our hearts beat wildly, as if we're being chased by those phantom guards with their phantom guns.

Once we make it to the safety of the forest on the other side, Mama lets us rest, but only for a moment, then we're off again, Pieta whimpering, and in her whisper voice complaining that she's tired, that she wants to go home. But Mama ignores her and presses on, until suddenly she stops.

"Here, I think," she says, pointing to a thick stand of linden trees, branches still so full that it's impossible to see what might be beyond. They smell like honey and lemon.

Mama leads us past to a large pile of rocks so blanketed with ivy and nettles and ground elder that it takes a minute to realize what it is: a stone cabin. Mama pulls enough vines away to expose an entrance, the door long since gone. She ducks inside and almost immediately vanishes into the darkness.

"Mama!" I yell, worried.

A light flares inside the cabin as Mama flicks on a small torch, and we can see in now after her—a floor covered with rotting leaves;

cobwebs everywhere; a roof half caved in, but still holding on one side, the heavy branch of a linden tree mostly covering the hole. Mama busies herself clearing the cobwebs, flushing a cluster of spiders, tossing out an empty bird nest. She grabs a leafy branch and sweeps out some small animal droppings, and I'm relieved once she tells us what it is. "So no bear, then?" I ask. "And no wild boar?"

Mama says no and, finished, invites us in with her. "There's not a lot of room," she says. "But enough for the three of us. Enough for the two of you if you ever need to come here."

"But what is this place?" I ask.

She shrugs. "When I was girl, my friends and I found it and made it our clubhouse. We used to come here all the time and pretend. Whenever we could sneak away from Opa and Oma. But I think they knew. They must have known."

She doesn't say much else. Just spreads a blanket on the dirt floor so we can sit, Pieta and I scooting as close to her as we can. Even though Mama has cleared it of debris, the cabin is still windowless and dark and scary.

"It may have been for hunters, if they became lost," Mama says. "But we never saw anyone here, so it must have been quite old and forgotten, even back then."

"But why are we here?" I ask. Pieta, wide-eyed, nods.

"In case something happens," Mama says. "We will come here and hide. And if I'm not at the farm for some reason, or Opa and

Oma, or the guards—in case of anything—you both are to stay together and come here on your own. Do you understand me, Asta? I want you to stay together, you and Pieta, and run, run, run. Remember the way here. On the way back to the farm, I'll show you landmarks to help you. And once you're here, stay until I come for you. Look after each other. You'll need to bring food and water and blankets. Bring whatever you can with you. It'll be winter soon. But no fires. Anyone looking will see the smoke and be able to find you." She thinks for a minute. "If there's no time, then you'll have to make do once you're here. Through the forest, to the west, is the river." She starts to say more but stops herself.

I want to ask her what might happen, but I already know. The Red Army, of course. If they were to come to the farm.

Mama takes my hand, then she takes Pieta's hand. "I promise you," she says, "if you come here, and if you wait for me, no matter how long it takes, I will come for you. I will take care of you. I will always, always look after you."

CHAPTER 6
PIETA

The soldiers have left! Oma is so happy she is baking pies to celebrate. I am helping her turn the dough into pie crusts with a wooden rolling pin. She says the Red Army has been chased back from Gumbinnen. Chased out of East Prussia and back across the border into Lithuania. She says the invasion is over.

But at dinner, before Oma serves dessert, Opa corrects her. "They will be back," he says. "The Red Army was only testing our defenses."

Everyone is quiet after that. I stare at my pie, not sure if I should eat it if Oma and Mama aren't going to eat theirs, but in the end, I do, and so does Asta.

That night in bed, Asta says maybe Opa is wrong. Maybe the Red Army will go around us. They still have Poland to conquer before mainland Germany. Why bother with East Prussia?

But I don't think she believes what she's saying. She's probably trying to make me feel better about things.

But I don't care about the Red Army. I'm just glad the soldiers have left. I was afraid they would eat the ducks the way they ate Opa's pigs and just about everything in Oma's larder and all the chickens' eggs and drank Opa's special beers. The workers were afraid when the soldiers were here. I could see it in their faces, in their eyes, their nervous eyes, always watching. No one on the farm would ever hurt the workers with their strange languages and their funny accents when they try to speak ours. I ask Asta one night why the workers were afraid of our soldiers.

"Because they are the enemy," she says. "The ones Papa is fighting."

"But I thought Papa was fighting the Red Army." Mama had told us this. She had gotten a letter from Papa. From the Soviet Union. But that was a long time ago.

"They are all the enemy," Asta says. "On both sides of us. The east and the west. The Red Army is coming from the east. Where Papa is. Or was."

I only remember Papa a little. And less and less every day. Asta misses him more than I do. She had him much longer. Mama never talks about Papa, but I think she must miss him the most of all. But when he comes home, when the war is over, I will know him better then. I will have more to remember. When the war is over, no one will miss anyone anymore.

CHAPTER 7
ASTA

Winter comes with snow, a light dusting at first, then harder in the days that follow as the workers are sent into the fields as soon as the sun crests the treetops. November is for reaping and threshing the wheat, oats, and barley, for baling the straw and stacking it to the rafters in Opa's cow sheds, and for the hard chore of digging up potatoes and sugar beets from ground that is already starting to freeze. The hardest job is digging up the sugar beets, which takes the longest and which everyone hates. Even Pieta and I go out with spades to help, though I think we're more a bother than anything.

By the end of November, everyone is so tired that the October invasion is all but forgotten. Most days now, Pieta and I wear cast-off trousers and boots under our sack dresses—everything too big for us, but we don't mind. Pant legs can be rolled up. Suspenders can be adjusted. Coat sleeves can be pinned. Boots can be stuffed with rags. Mama says Pieta and I look like real farm girls now.

It makes Oma unhappy. She thinks that we should dress like we did in the city, like proper girls, proper the way the Führer has ordered, anyway, even here on the farm where there's no one to see us, no block wardens to report infractions to the authorities, the way they reported anyone who forgot to greet others with "Heil Hitler!" In Königsberg, we must have said it a hundred times a day, with right arms raised just so, to neighbors, black shirts, soldiers, officers, teachers, shopkeepers, even our friends.

I always remembered, of course. I never wanted to get into trouble, or to cause trouble for Mama. In school I did all my work—neatly, correctly, and on time. But Pieta, she was the forgetful one, always distracted, always having to be reminded. For some reason our Blockwart, an elderly man who was suspicious of everyone, who would report the slightest infraction of Nazi Party rules, never seemed to tire of reminding Pieta when she forgot to Heil, and in a gentle voice that I never heard him use with anyone else. I was afraid of the Blockwart. Everyone was. But Pieta would just smile when he corrected her. She would lift her right arm, but more as if to wave than to salute. And she would mouth the words *Heil Hitler*, but I'm not sure she ever said them out loud.

On Sundays, Opa gathers everyone in the barn, including some of the neighbors. Hymns are sung. Bible passages are read. Prayers are offered. In Königsberg we stopped going to church after the

Blockwart told everyone that the party now officially disapproved. He said Hitler had made a speech, had made many speeches, saying that Christianity was a religion fit only for slaves and not suitable for proud German people. Proud Germans, Hitler said— the Übermensch—believed in the natural law of survival of the fittest; we bowed and prayed to no one.

But in Opa and Oma's barn, it is different. As we huddle together in prayer—even the Allied prisoners—I think we are like the New Testament shepherds, keeping watch over our flocks by night, summoned to the manger in Bethlehem on Christmas to await the coming of the baby Jesus.

We do this on Christmas Day, a snowy Monday. All week, Mama has had Pieta and me rehearsing "Stille Nacht," which we are to sing for Opa's service in the barn, and all week, Pieta has only pretended to sing with me, only mouthing the words and so forcing me to make up for her absence by being louder. Mama, too, pretends, says nothing to Pieta, only encouraging both of us, as if what has turned out to be my solo is still a duet: "Wonderful, girls. Now again."

It is no different when we're in the barn. First, Oma reads a handful of Christmas cards that have managed to come through the mail, saving for last a special letter from Mama's favorite cousin, Gretta, who lives in a village near Hamburg, inviting us to come stay with them. Then Opa reads the Christmas story from the Book of Luke.

Mama nudges us forward when he finishes, our feet rustling on the straw-strewn floor. I take Pieta's hand, thinking it will comfort her, and perhaps encourage her enough that she will actually join me. I smile politely to the prisoners and the guards and the neighbors, all of whom have made the trek this Christmas morning to Opa and Oma's farm, and I close my eyes and begin my very best "Silent Night."

At first I'm all alone, but then, in the second verse, I hear a small voice, so faint that I may be the only one who can. But it doesn't matter, because it's Pieta after all, letting me know that she's still here with me, and it's how we carry each other through to the end.

CHAPTER 8
PIETA

I ask Mama about her cousin Gretta, the one in the village who wrote the Christmas letter. Asta wants to know about her, too.

"Why did she invite us to stay with them?" I ask. "Isn't Hamburg so far away?"

Mama says Oma has a sister we have never met, and the sister's daughter is Gretta, who is Mama's same age.

"I visited them once," Mama says. "Long before you were born. Even before Papa and I were married. When I still lived at home with Oma and Opa."

"What does their house look like?" Asta wants to know. "Does Gretta have children our ages, and are they boys or girls?"

"A boy and a girl," Mama says. "Johan and Tilda. Oma's sister lives with Gretta and her husband, too. I remember when Gretta was a girl and had twin ponies they kept in a small pen in their yard, and they let me ride one all by myself, even though I was little. And the house they lived in, it looked like a gingerbread house."

Asta has a hundred other questions, the way she always does. And does Mama think we can visit them someday, since they invited us, and since the war will be over soon?

I only want to know if they still have the ponies, and if I can ride them, and if they're nice, and if we can stay in their gingerbread house, too.

CHAPTER 9
ASTA

The New Year starts off with good news. The order has come down from the High Command that the evacuation of East Prussia will begin soon, before the end of the month, before the Red Army has time to attack us again. No one has been allowed to leave East Prussia before now, even though Mama says everyone has known for months that Germany will lose the war.

Opa tells us this as we're standing in the kitchen. He says we are to help drive all the livestock from the farm to Gumbinnen first—to be loaded onto trains and taken to somewhere inside what is left of Mainland Germany. Then we will go.

"No one will be left behind to face the Soviets," Opa says. "The High Command has promised us this. And those who can't find room on the trains through Poland will be boarded onto ships at Gotenhafen and the other port cities on the Baltic. But that's too far away for us. So—the trains. We can only pray that they have not waited until it is too late."

Even as he says this, Opa seems doubtful. Mama and Oma look at each other and shake their heads. Pieta busies herself with small bits of cloth and a needle and thread. She is making a dress for one of the ducks. I think she is so ridiculous sometimes, but maybe because it's New Year's Day, Oma is even helping her.

"But what about the soldiers who guard the farm?" I ask. "Will they also come with us on the train?"

Opa shakes his head. "It is the duty of the Wehrmacht to protect us," he says. "They will stay and fight the Soviets to give the citizens time to escape. That is the order."

"They will be evacuated, too, won't they?" I ask. "As soon as they know we are safe. They won't be left behind?"

"Of course not," Mama says, when she realizes Opa isn't responding. He is staring out the window at the snow drifts that the wind blew against the barn overnight. Or maybe he's not staring at anything, only thinking. "The soldiers will follow us to safety, of course they will, but they have their job to do, just as we have our jobs to do. Herding the cattle. Loading the wagons with the stores of winter food. People must eat, and it is still our job to feed them, even if we have to leave."

Opa asks me what the rest of Germany calls East Prussia, and I dutifully answer what we were taught in school: "The Breadbasket of the German Reich." Even Pieta mumbles it; we've been ordered to say it so many times.

"And what about the Allied prisoners who work on the farm?" I ask. "What will happen to them?"

It is Oma who answers this time, looking up from the floor where she's sitting on the bear rug with Pieta and the duck dress. "They will stay here. Or they will leave. They will belong to the Red Army after we're gone. But we mustn't say anything to them. They will need to help load the wagons and herd and slaughter the livestock. There is much to be done."

She seems sad. I'm sad, too. We already are without Papa, who we haven't seen in two years. We left Königsberg during the bombing six months ago and haven't had any letters from him since. Now we have to say goodbye to the farm where Mama grew up with Opa and Oma, and where we've been living since Königsberg. All my life, I have known no other places in East Prussia—only the Baltic Sea where we used to go sometimes in the summer and the Memel Forest where we stayed in a cabin when I was little. All before the war.

But there's no time to worry about all that today. Opa has another announcement. "As soon as the breakfast dishes have been cleared," he says, "it is time for the hunt."

He says this as if we know what he's talking about. Mama sighs, so she clearly does. Oma pulls herself up and goes into the kitchen.

It has been a lazy morning so far, and I'd thought it was going to stay that way, like another Christmas Day. But now there's this thing—this hunt. And we're told to bundle up because we're going to meet up with other farm families in the area.

Mama rolls her eyes. "It's the tradition," she says as she shoves mittens on our hands, and stuffs rags into our oversized boots, and wraps scarves around and around our necks and over ours mouths and noses, and two jackets each. Soon all I can see of Pieta and all Pieta can see of me are our eyes. We beg Mama to say more about where we're going, but she just tells us to hurry along. "You will see soon enough when we get there." And then she shoves us out the door and into the frozen day.

Opa and Mama have to lift us onto the wagon after we wade through the snow outside and over to the barn. The horses' heads are surrounded by clouds of their steamy breaths. We settle into a nest of straw and wait there, already shivering, until Mama and Oma join us. They bury us under blankets, and then off we go down the winter roads to meet the others for this mysterious hunt.

CHAPTER 10
PIETA

I don't mind the cold as much as Asta does, even though I'm younger. I know she thinks she's supposed to look after me, and I can be forgetful sometimes, it's true. But I let her lean against me in the hay wagon because I can look after her, too, when she's shivering like now—even though she'll never admit that she is. And anyway, after a bumpy hour on the snowy roads we're there, although *there* just seems like everywhere else to me at first. More forest. More snow. More gray winter sky. More cold. Except when I look deeper into the woods where we turn off the road, I see them—more wagons and more horses stamping their feet and snorting. The horses have blankets of their own tied on their backs, and when our wagons stop next to them, Opa and the workers tie blankets on our horses, too. That makes me happy. I was worried that they would be cold like Asta, and they wouldn't have someone like me to warm them up.

"Here you go, girls," Mama says, and she hands us pots and pans and big spoons Oma uses for cooking. The workers line up, too, stamping their feet like the horses while waiting for their pots and pans and spoons. At the other wagons it's the same. Opa and Rolf and our other soldiers and the rest of the men pull hunting rifles and ammunition from boxes under the seats in the wagons. They sling game bags over their shoulders and hang big knives on belts outside their heavy coats.

Mama tells us to follow her and Oma, and she signals to the workers as well, so off we go, wading through the snow and even farther into the woods. The other women, children, and workers follow. A girl named Johanna waves at Asta and me, and we wave back with our pots and pans. I bang mine together until Mama shushes me. "Not yet, Pieta. Not until I tell you." Johanna laughs, and I'm embarrassed. But I pretend to laugh, too, because I don't think she means to make fun of me. She once drew a picture of one of my ducklings and gave it to me. She signed it, too, like a real artist. Mama let me tack it to the wall above our bed in the attic.

I don't want to be here. The snow is up to our knees. Some of the trees are bare, but some of them are evergreens and are pretty with their needles so fresh you can even smell them in the still air. It's not the cold that bothers me. It's what is about to happen.

"We are making a giant circle," Mama explains. "Oma and I will continue ahead, but we won't be far. The other families and their workers went in the other direction. Once the two halves of the circle meet, then I will be the one who blows the whistle. See?" She pulls free a shiny silver whistle that's been hiding under her scarf. "When you hear the whistle, everyone will start walking forward and banging with the pots and pans and spoons. There is a clearing at the center of the circle and Opa and the other farmers and the soldiers are there with their guns. Waiting."

"Waiting for what?" Asta asks. But I already know. I saw a hare running away through the snow. Maybe he knew what was going to happen, too. I'm glad he escaped. I wish all the animals could escape.

"If we're lucky, we will flush out more rabbits and hares and chase them toward Opa and the men," Mama says. "And if we're very lucky, there will also be deer and wild boar for them to shoot, for a New Year's feast this afternoon. The animals will run away from us—away from the noise we make. It will startle them, and they'll only have the one direction to go."

Of all the questions to ask, Asta only wants to know what's the difference between a rabbit and a hare. I could tell her, but I can't find my voice today. Like most days. Hares have longer ears and longer legs. They run faster. Rabbits like to hide. Hares are better at running away from danger. Today, it would be better to be a rabbit, I think. I wish there were only rabbits, and they would all hide from the hunt.

After Mama and Oma leave us, Asta tells me to keep stamping my feet like the horses and the prisoners to help keep warm. I already know this. I don't like it when she calls them "prisoners," but I don't say anything. I hate the metal feel of the pot I'm holding in one hand and Oma's frying pan in the other. Even through my mittens. They make me think I'm one of the hunters, too, holding something like a gun.

For a few more minutes the forest is still, and then we hear the shrill whistle followed by the awful noise of the clanging pots and pans, not just ours but dozens of them echoing all around us in the woods. It hurts my ears, even though I refuse to bang mine like Asta and like everyone else. I'm only glad that so far I don't hear any of the guns, and I don't see any deer or boar or rabbits or even hares running away from us and toward Opa and the men.

The circle tightens like a noose. I see others on either side of us now through the trees as we're closing in. And then I hear it—guns firing. One, then two, then more. And as soon as I think it has stopped, it starts again. I drop my frying pan and my cooking pot and cover my ears with my mittens, but the shooting continues, and Asta and the others keep marching forward, and I follow. Asta doesn't notice what I'm doing, or what I'm not doing. She is staring straight ahead. Asta always follows the orders she is given. She always does her proper duty. I know I should be that way, too, but sometimes I just can't.

I see, through the trees, in the closing circle, Johanna, who like

Asta is marching forward. I wonder how she can draw a duckling with every feather in place, the tiny bill, the webbed feet just so— and then do this awful thing? How can any of us? Mama would tell me I'm being silly and we are to be grateful for what we have and not complain. Only I don't feel that way and I want to tell Mama that, and tell Asta, and even tell Johanna, but when I look over to her again, Johanna isn't there. She has fallen into the snow. She tries to get up but only rises to her knees. There is blood spreading down her coat from her shoulder, splashing onto the snow. She looks at the stain, then falls again face down into the red snow and this time she doesn't get back up, not even to her knees. She doesn't move at all. Asta sees this, too. I scream and start to run to the fallen Joanna until Asta clutches my arm. It is already too late.

There is more shooting, and I finally realize it is coming from behind us. From all around us. Afraid, I step closer to Asta. Through the forest we see soldiers emerging from the trees, soldiers in fur caps with red stars on the front, soldiers in heavy coats and boots, soldiers with guns, rushing toward us through the snow, firing their weapons. I think I see tongues of flame coming out of the barrels.

"The Red Army!" Asta shouts. "They're back!"

A woman kneels beside Joanna's fallen body, but only for a second until someone else grabs her arm and pulls her up, the way Asta has hold of my arm. They are running through the snow, trying to get away. Asta and I are running, too, at first toward the wagons, but when we see more of the soldiers there, Asta drags me in a different direction, and we wade through snow drifts deeper into the woods. We're like the hares. Asta is determined to get us away from the shooting. We see others fall. We see more splashes of red staining the white snow. I look for Mama and Oma but don't see them anywhere. I can't hear anything except the guns, the guns, the guns. It feels as though we're back in Königsberg during the bombing. Everything is shaking, exploding, threatening to fall apart. Only this is different. Only this is the same.

CHAPTER II
ASTA

The Red Army is everywhere. No matter what direction we go, there are more soldiers. We stop and hide. We bury ourselves in the snow, afraid to breathe until they pass. We wade even deeper into the forest. We go in the wrong direction, toward them, hoping to come out behind them, to where they were but where we hope they aren't anymore. But I don't know where else to go except back to the farm. I pray the soldiers haven't found it yet. I pray that Mama and Opa and Oma will be there.

I don't let go of Pieta the whole time. I know that if I do, she'll run back to the hunt to look for Mama and Oma and Opa, the way a horse will run back inside a burning barn if you don't hold it back. I worry about what she might find if she goes. I can't think about what's back there. I shake my head to make the thoughts go away— of Johanna lying in the red snow, of a soldier who looked right at me as he took aim with his rifle, and then lifted his head and turned to speak to his comrade, and then aimed somewhere else instead. Aimed at someone else. I saw him pull the trigger. I heard the explosion. I heard another sound, of something hit, and screaming, and crying. The crying was me.

There is no one at the farm. We stumble to the barn, exhausted, frozen, numb. And still afraid. We peek inside but can't see anything it's so dark. But we hear the cows and their lowing sounds. We hear the horses pacing in their stalls. Pieta inches forward, slips inside the barn door, and I follow her. It's warmer here—from the bodies of the farm animals, from the sturdy walls blocking the wind and the snow. We collapse on a bed of straw and neither of us moves for the longest time. We only rouse ourselves because of thirst and hunger and the realization that, even in the warmer barn, it's still too cold for us to stay.

We cross the frozen yard to the house, grateful, and still surprised, that the Red Army soldiers haven't been here, that nothing has been touched, or burned, or destroyed, or slaughtered. We let ourselves in— quietly, stealthily—not lighting any lanterns or candles, only stoking the embers of the morning fire a little in the fireplace and huddling close to the heat. Once I can feel my hands again, I go to the kitchen for bread and cheese and sausage and sauerkraut and carrots—whatever I can find.

We drink straight from the water pitcher and eat with our hands, like starved children, though it's only been since this morning that we last ate. But anything to keep from thinking about what happened, about what we left behind us. Anything to keep from worrying about Mama and Opa and Oma and the rest. I need to be strong. I tell myself this over and over. Pieta needs me to be strong. Mama would want me to be strong, to take care of Pieta, to not be afraid.

"We can't stay here," I tell Pieta. "We have to pack up whatever we can and go to Mama's shelter."

She nods. But neither of us moves, and I think of all the reasons I can for us to stay instead. It's warm here. Mama might come back. Opa and Oma, too. The farmers and the guards have guns. They could stop the Red Army soldiers. Chase them off. Maybe the soldiers aren't so many. Maybe they are a lost patrol. Maybe they took a wrong turn. Maybe it's still not the real invasion. And it's night already, and there's only a trace of moon. And it's freezing. And there's so much snow in the forest, so much snow everywhere. Could we even find our way back to the cabin, especially now? Could I remember the landmarks Mama showed us? Would we get lost? And how will we carry what we need? Blankets and extra clothes and food and a knife and an ax. And what if all the pots and pans are gone from Oma's kitchen, scattered now in the forest where we brought them, and where they were dropped when the shooting started at the hunt, when the Red Army came? What will we bring to cook in? To heat water? To do anything? We've never been on our own. Never. Never.

"Asta?" Pieta says.

That's all. Just my name. A question. And I get up to start packing everything I can think of that we'll need to survive now that the war has found us again.

CHAPTER 12
PIETA

Asta finds two sacks and busies herself filling them with food while I gather as many blankets as I can carry downstairs from the bedrooms. I find the duck dress Oma and I were sewing. It's not finished, but I tuck it into my pocket anyway.

Asta tells me to go to the barn and get one of the horses, so I bundle myself back up and cross the quiet yard again and pick out my favorite, a Black Forest horse named Fedde. He's smaller than the other draft horses, so we might be able to climb on his back if he'll let us. He's very strong, even for his size, and Opa lets me feed him and comb him sometimes. Fedde's coat is a dark chestnut color, and he has a long flaxen mane and tail the color of straw, and he's beautiful and he's also handsome. A two-tone horse. I find a heavy blanket and throw it over his back and tie it on. Then I fit the halter over his head and secure it the way I've seen Opa do a hundred times.

I shovel as much grain as I can into two feed bags that I tie together so one hangs on each side of him. I stop for a minute, leave him standing, waiting in his stall while I find my way across the dark barn to a wooden ramp that takes me to the loft and a duck pen Opa had the workers build there for the winter. I watch them sleeping, the whole duck family tucked into one another, and it makes me happy. I don't want to wake them. I had an idea that I would put the dress on one of the ducklings, but instead I leave it inside the pen, not that I expect them to know what it is. But in the morning, they will find it and peck at it and try to figure out what it is. A surprise.

But I can't stay any longer. Asta will be angry with me if she knows what I've been doing. I climb down the ramp and feel my way back to the horse stalls, then I attach a long rope to Fedde's halter and lead him out of the barn and back over to the house. His hooves make a chuffing sound in the soft snow.

· · · · · · · · · · ·

At first, Asta insists that I ride, even though I'm worried that Fedde will get too tired carrying me along with the heavy bags of feed and the bulky sacks that Asta has filled and tied on as well. But I'm so sleepy when we set out that I don't argue. I wrap myself in blankets and lean all the way forward. I press my face against the back of Fedde's warm neck, cushioned by his soft mane. Asta wraps the rope around her hand and leads us away from the barn and through the fallow fields under a half-moon sky. I never fall asleep, even as tired as I am. I'm afraid of falling off. I'm afraid something will happen. I watch Asta through my half-shut eyes, and she never wavers.

I don't know how she remembers the landmarks, but she does. A fence post. A copse of trees. A hill. A rock formation. The direction of the moon. Fedde slogs through the snow as if it's water, or as if it's nothing. It's almost as if he knows where we're going, too. After a long time—An hour? Two hours?—I pull off the blankets and climb down from Fedde's back.

"You ride," I say to Asta, but she just shakes her head.

"I'm bigger than you," she says. "I don't want to wear him out." So we walk together. I would be lost without Asta. I know this. I wouldn't know my way. She must know this, too, and that's the real reason she won't ride, even though she's so tired now that her steps seem to hardly take her forward. But she won't stop. She says we can't. It's not safe.

"We need it to snow," she says.

"Why?" I ask. "There's too much now. And it's so cold."

Asta looks behind us and points at our tracks—hers and mine and Fedde's—and I understand. I look up at the sky, but there's still just the lonely half-moon and the far, faraway stars.

I still don't want it to snow, though, because then how will we ever find the cabin? How will Mama find us? How will we stay warm when we get there? Already I'm afraid. If it starts snowing, I don't know what I'll do.

But that's not true. Because I do know. I will always follow Asta no matter what.

CHAPTER 13
ASTA

We walk right past it at first. Then circle around it. I know we're close, but I've been staring at everything so hard for so long in the hours it takes to get here from the farm, looking for landmarks in the dark, anxious about missing signs that might be buried under the snow, worrying about getting us lost, that once we make it, I'm not able to see what's right in front of me. Until it suddenly materializes, like magic, and Pieta whispers, "Oh. Here." We've practically stumbled into it.

I only keep the torch on for a little bit as we sweep out the snow. I make Pieta stay inside while I cut boughs with soft needles from fir trees the way Mama told us she used to do when she was a girl. We lay those on the damp floor for our bed and cover it with Fedde's thick horse blanket. Pieta protests. She wants me to leave the horse blanket on Fedde since we have to tie him to one of the trees outside, but I promise her he'll be all right, that the tree will provide him with enough shelter. She eventually gives in, too tired to argue anymore. I coax her back in and get her to lie down on the bed we've made so I can cover her up with all the other blankets. I tell her that Mama will be here in the morning—I'm sure of it.

Pieta falls asleep right away, but I'm still wide-awake. I jump at every sound. A creaking branch. A falling icicle. An owl. The wind. The whistling sound Pieta makes through her nose every time she exhales. My mind won't stop spinning from worry. What if Fedde *is* too cold outside? What if he dies in the night? What if we freeze as well—even with all the blankets in the cabin? I wish I could build a fire, but Mama said not to, that someone might see. But who? Surely no one followed us here, and now it's snowing—not a lot, but enough to cover our tracks from the farm. I check on Fedde one last time, then crawl under the blankets with Pieta. We're both wearing all our clothes, our mittens, our boots, our coats and scarves and knit caps and hoods.

It's so dark in here with no windows and the moon now low in the sky. Snowflakes drift through the hole in the half-fallen roof. I can't see them. I can only feel them landing softly on my face. I bury my head under the blankets and press myself closer to Pieta and pray for sleep. But my mind still won't let me. It can't be quiet. I keep worrying that the Red Army has captured Mama and Opa and Oma and Rolf and the others. Or worse than captured. Like Johanna. And then what will we do? We've already lost Papa to the war. Our home in Königsberg. Everything. How can we live without Mama?

CHAPTER 14
PIETA

I wake up before Asta. It's still dark inside the shelter, but enough gray light filters through the hole in the roof that I can see to pull myself free of the tangle of blankets. The shock of the cold makes me want to dive right back under, but I force myself outside. I have to check on Fedde and feed him. I lift one of the heavy sacks of grain that we piled with everything else to barricade ourselves in where the missing door is supposed to be. I don't see Fedde, not at first, but then I do: not standing where we left him, but lying on his side, half covered in snow, the rope pulled taut, holding his head at an awkward angle. I run to him, my heart pounding, afraid he's dead, afraid we killed him by making him stay out all night in the cold and the snow. I throw myself on him, brush the snow away as fast as I can, as if that will help, and maybe it does, or maybe it's just the thing that rouses him, because he shakes his head and snorts and struggles to his feet and stamps his hooves on the ground and whinnies. I hug his neck and kiss his long nose, and he whinnies again and stamps around some more.

I scoop a bowl in the snow and fill it with grain. Fedde is so hungry that he nudges me out of the way with his head to get to it. I brush more snow off his back and wish I had thought to bring his brush and comb to untangle his mane. I'm trying to work out some of the knots with my frozen fingers when Asta joins me. She looks all around us at the frozen forest. It's as if she's expecting something. Or someone. Mama. Asta starts crying. I'm supposed to be the one who cries, not her. Tears freeze on her face. I want to make things better, but all I can think to do is brush off her cheeks with my mittens. They're crusted with dirt and snow and I only manage to make a mess of things.

· · · · · · · · · · ·

It's too cold to stay out long, and soon we're back inside the shelter, huddled under all the blankets, nibbling on cheese and bread and sausage. Asta says, "Only a little, Pieta. We don't know how long we have to make it last." We're staring at an apple, wondering if we can afford to eat that now, too. And that's when we hear something.

Asta goes tearing out of the shelter, tripping over the sacks at the entrance and sprawling into the snow, certain that it's Mama. I follow, but not so sure. What if it's someone else? But Mama sings out to us, shouts Asta's name, and asks "Where is Pieta?" I am immediately bursting with happiness and relief!

I pop my head out of the shelter so she can see me. She's on the ground hugging Asta, who is crying again, and now I'm crying, too. It's a pile of us falling all over one another. Even Fedde pulls as close as he can, straining against the rope. I stroke his long nose and wish I had the apple for him. Mama and Asta are both talking at once, asking each other questions, too excited to answer until Mama picks herself up and shoos us back inside the shelter where it's warmer and drier, though not so much until we're all three under blankets.

Asta has collected snow in one of Oma's pots, one of the few left behind on the hunt. She covers it and keeps it under the blanket with us until it melts, then she gives it to Mama who drinks half before offering it back to us so we can drink, too. I break off some of the black bread and hand Mama the rest of the food we have out—the sausage and cheese and the one apple. Mama is famished and she eats and we watch her and wait to find out what happened at the hunt after we ran away, after the shooting began. I see dried blood crusted to her coat, down her sleeves. Her clothes are torn and dirty. She has scratches on her face. Her hands, freed from her mittens, are shaking. She's halfway through a bite of bread when she puts down the food. Asta fixes a blanket higher on Mama's shoulders and tries to tuck it around her, but Mama shrugs it off. She reaches for our hands.

"I'm so sorry," she says. "Opa and Oma are gone."

CHAPTER 15
ASTA

Mama won't tell us what happened, though I keep asking until she snaps at me, and then she says she's sorry again, and then I stop asking. Pieta won't let go of Mama's hand until Mama pries her loose, and even then it's for only a second—to relieve herself outside, to gather more pine boughs, to check on Fedde. Mama piles sticks and logs and branches, as much as she can find, to make Fedde a stall. That's what Mama calls it, but it's not really a stall. Fedde could step right over it if he wasn't still tied to the tree. But Mama says it's protection from the night wind when Fedde lies down later. She tells us that horses don't get cold in their hooves and their legs, which is why they can stand in the snow and not be too bothered. She says when they stand, they rest one leg at a time, shifting their weight to the other three. And they can sleep standing up, like I told Pieta, but sometimes they need to lie down for awhile, too.

Mama tries to keep us busy, but there's only so much we can do. She does her best to cover the opening in the half-fallen roof with more branches she cuts down with the ax I brought. I wish she would build a fire, but she still says no. Someone might see. Someone might find us. It's not safe, even here. I can see how tired she is. How weary. And how sad. I'm sad, too. And cold, even under all the blankets. And scared. I couldn't be afraid when I had to take care of Pieta, but now that Mama is here, I can't help it. I want to go home. I want to be warm. I want to see Opa and Oma and everyone. I want everything to be just the way it was before. I can't think about Königsberg, but I can't stop thinking about the farm and all the animals in the barn and Oma's kitchen and all of us sitting around the fireplace and Mama sending Pieta and me off to bed in the attic and us stopping halfway, eavesdropping on the grown-ups and Opa's radio and their low voices in serious talk and their laughter about Pieta and her ducklings.

"Can't we go back to the farm?" I ask Mama. "No one came when we were there. No soldiers. Not anyone."

"We can't go back there. Not ever."

"Then where?" I ask, my voice trembling. Pieta is practically sitting in Mama's lap, her eyes wide. "The train in Gumbinnen?"

But Mama shakes her head. "That way will be too dangerous. The Red Army soldiers may be there already, and who knows if the trains are still running. We will have to go north, to the Baltic. Opa said there will be ships there for the evacuation."

She is silent. I wonder if these are things Opa said to Mama at the end, after the shooting. I wonder if that is Opa's blood on Mama's coat. I miss Opa and Oma so much, and my chest hurts from the sadness I feel. I pray they didn't suffer.

Darkness falls early in the Romincka Forest. Mama does a much better job of covering the entrance to the shelter, packing snow into a half wall to keep out the wind. Pieta is worried that Fedde will be lonely if he can't see us, but Mama assures her that he will know we're still here. It's almost cozy now inside, but once Mama turns off her flashlight, I feel a rising panic. It was like this in the shelter in Königsberg during the bombing when the lights went out. The whole world shook so violently that I was certain the building standing over us would collapse. Some of the buildings did—many, many of them—but not ours.

I reach out for Mama and feel her arm and hold onto her like Pieta. I press myself against her back under the blankets and can feel her heartbeat, even there.

CHAPTER 16
PIETA

We walk and walk and walk and walk. Mama ties two ropes to Fedde and gives each of us one end on either side. She says to hold on and he will help us through the snow drifts and so we do. Sweet Fedde is working so hard. He pulls us along behind Mama. Mama leads the way through the forest. I don't know how she knows where to go. The sky is gray. There is snow everywhere. It all looks the same. Nothing changes. We stop at a stream and Mama chops a hole in the ice with the ax. First we let Fedde drink. He drinks for a long, long time. Mama says horses need more water when it's cold, and eating snow isn't enough. It's not enough for people, either, and when Fedde is finished, we drink cup after cup after cup. We're hungry, but Mama will only let us eat a little at a time. The bread and cheese are so hard it hurts my jaw to chew. I try to hold every bite in my mouth long enough for it to soften, but my stomach tells me to chew and swallow faster and so I do. My stomach hurts. I don't complain. We keep walking through the snow. I wish there wasn't so much snow. I wish there wasn't any snow. I wish we were back at Opa and Oma's farm and I was playing with my ducklings. I hope they're all right. I hope someone else is at the farm and is taking good care of them. I hope it's Opa and Oma back on the farm. Mama didn't say the soldiers shot them like they shot Johanna. She only said they were gone. But they could be gone back to the farm, and why not?

In the afternoon there is a faint circle in the sky and Mama says, "Look! The sun!" She says it is a sign of good things. A sign that we're going the right way. A sign that everything is going to be all right for us. The faint circle fades. We keep walking. I stumble. I stumble again. I hold tightly to the rope like Mama said, and so I don't fall all the way down, but it hurts anyway.

I ask Mama if I can please ride Fredde.

"I'm sorry," Mama says. "But he is tired, just like we are."

She repacks all our bags so they lay more evenly on his back, but he's still working hard to carry everything and to pull Asta and me through the snow drifts.

"Isn't there a road?" Asta asks.

Mama shakes her head. "Not yet. Not until we get farther north, out of reach of the Red Army soldiers."

Asta keeps pressing. "But how will we know when we're far enough?"

"Maybe in a few days," Mama says. "When it's safe, we can find a road. Or maybe we can find someone else with a wagon who will let us ride."

No one speaks for awhile. We plod through the snow. Sometimes we stop to rest, but only for a few minutes. When Asta catches her breath, she asks Mama more questions: "How far is it to the coast? How far to Gotenhafen? How far to the Baltic?"

Mama says, "It all depends," but she won't say what it depends on, so I have to guess: It depends on how much snow. It depends on if we get lost. It depends on Fedde. It depends on how tired Asta and I get. It depends on whether we run into more soldiers. It depends on finding the road soon. It depends on the kindness of strangers.

Mama says we'll stop here for the night, but I look around and there's no shelter, no cabin, no farm, nowhere to stay, only snow, snow, snow. Mama points to a fallen tree and says, "There." I still don't understand until she leads us over and starts digging with her hands next to the trunk. She tells Asta and me to help and we start digging, too, though our hands are already frozen, even inside our mittens. I have to stop and shove my hands between my legs and squeeze tightly down on them to get them warm again, to get the feeling back, and then I can dig some more until I have to stop and thaw them out again.

We're digging a snow cave—I can see that now, with the tree trunk for shelter on one side. When it's deep enough, Mama sends us off to gather pine boughs to line the bottom. She covers them with the horse blanket. She fixes two bed blankets over us after we climb inside and it's cozier than I thought, even warm once our body heat is trapped inside.

Asta hugs Mama. "I wish I had grown up on a farm, too," she says. "And then I would know as much as you about these things."

Mama hugs Asta back. She hugs both of us. "You've already done such a good job of figuring out how to survive," she says.

She tells Asta how proud she is of her for taking care of us when we ran away from the shooting and made our way back to the farm and then to the secret shelter. She says she's proud of me, too, and she gives me my ration of bread and cheese and sausage and then divides an apple for us all to share.

I'm so tired I can hardly keep my eyes open. Asta is the same. I mean to ask Mama about Fedde, will he be all right here, another night outside and alone in the snow, but I fall asleep too fast.

CHAPTER 17
ASTA

We have run out of food. After four days we are still in the Romincka Forest, still wading through snow, and it has begun snowing again. When we wake up after the fourth night, our shelter is buried. The blanket Mama fixed over us for cover is all that is between us and a heavy foot of snow. We have to dig ourselves out, and the whole time Pieta and I are worried that Fedde has been buried, too. But there he is, standing, waiting patiently. He shakes off the falling snow as soon as it lands. He has stamped out a space for himself under a tree, and when the branches get too heavy and drop their snowy load on top of him, he shakes that off, too. Pieta goes to him anyway and hugs his neck and whispers to him and strokes his long nose. She scoops a couple handfuls of grain for Fedde out of the last bag of feed, and I'm tempted to steal some.

Mama eats a handful of snow, and another and another. She tells me to eat some, too. But my stomach hurts and my teeth freeze. We drag our sacks of clothes and blankets out of the hole. Mama ties everything back on Fedde. I'm not much help. My fingers are already numb from the cold. My mittens get in the way. I snap at Pieta, who is no help at all, but Mama tells me to stop. Pieta sticks out her tongue at me when Mama isn't looking. I want to slap her. She's such a child.

"Come," Mama says. "We have to go."

I know I shouldn't ask her, "How much farther?" but I can't help myself. I'm cold and tired and hungry and sad about losing Opa and Oma and leaving the farm, and afraid of what could be hiding behind every tree, and afraid of who might be behind us and gaining ground if we don't hurry—if we don't reach Gotenhafen soon.

But it won't be soon. Mama sighs and says, "From Gumbinnen to Gotenhafen by road is more than three hundred kilometers. We started out closer than Gumbinnen, but here in the forest, here in the snow . . ."

She doesn't finish. She doesn't have to. Pieta leans her head against Fedde. She doesn't move. I can't make myself move, either, not until Mama stirs. She hands me my rope, loops it around one of my mittens and bends my fingers to grasp it, then she hands Pieta hers and does the same thing. She swats Fedde lightly on his rump, and he plods forward and with the ropes so tightly wound around our hands, we are forced to plod forward with him.

The only good thing this morning is that the snow lets up after we begin walking. And when we stop to rest Mama says, "I think it will be safe now to turn east and find our way out of the Romincka Forest. There will be a road that we can follow to the coast."

"And then a ship?" I ask.

Mama nods. "When we reach Mainland Germany or perhaps a port in Norway, we will find a way to Hamburg and Gretta."

"Do they know we'll be coming?" I ask. "Won't it be rude for us to just show up at their door?"

Mama laughs. "It is war, Asta," she says. "I am certain they will understand and open up their home to us. All over Germany they are preparing. For so many years East Prussia has fed them and the soldiers in the Wehrmacht. And now it is their turn to set a place for us at their table, yes?"

My empty stomach rumbles at this talk about being fed and places at the table. I eat some more snow to quiet it down. Pieta has been listening, and the talk must have affected her the same way, because she takes two handfuls and eats her snow, too.

CHAPTER 18
PIETA

On the fifth day wading through snow in the forest, I ask Mama to let me ride on Fedde, but she says no. I'm hungry and tired and sad, and I don't think I can go any farther. I stop walking and just stand by myself as they continue, hardly noticing. Until finally they do.

Mama leaves Asta with Fedde and comes back. "I can carry you," she says. "For a little while. But we can't ask too much from Fedde."

I want to say yes, but I'm afraid she would fall down. She's carrying so much already. She's carrying Opa and Oma inside her. She's carrying Papa.

"That's okay, Mama. I'll be all right," I whisper.

"It won't be long now," she says. "The road can't be much farther."

I know she's only saying that so I will keep going. And I know I shouldn't have asked to ride Fedde. He can hardly lift his head as he walks. And whenever we stop, he lies down in the snow. I worry that he won't be able to get back up, but Mama makes him. Sometimes she has to hit him and I hate it when she does, but I don't say anything. I see Asta with tears in her eyes, watching it, but not enough tears anymore to cry. I'm the same way, I think. The tears are still there, but just not enough.

We hear the road before we see it. The tramping of boots, the rumbling of wagon wheels, the clopping of horses' hooves. Even Fedde perks up and practically dances now through the snow. Soon we see men pulling carts piled high with children and belongings. Herds of cows and goats. Dogs running in and out of people and their things. They hardly notice us when we step out of the woods and climb the embankment to the road. We stand to the side for a few minutes, as if we haven't seen people before, or not for a long, long time instead of just five days. But they have been such quiet days, our time in the Romincka Forest, that sometimes I wondered if the world might have changed when we came back into it. And it *has* changed. All these people on the road, their heads bowed like Fedde, all their sad faces. Did they lose their opa and oma, too, I wonder?

A dog comes up to me and rubs against my legs. I bend down to pet him, but someone in the line of people yells at him and he lifts his head and runs back into the stream. I see a girl who might be my age, or Asta's. She's sitting on a cart and holding a baby. I don't see their mother. Only a man, their father, straining forward, gripping the two handles of the cart and pulling as if he is one of Opa's draft horses. Something is wrong with the man. One of his legs is so stiff it hardly bends. I wave to the girl, but she only looks at me and doesn't wave back, doesn't say anything, doesn't even blink.

Mama has us fall in line behind them. She speaks to the father. He grunts, still straining to pull the cart. Still limping with his stiff leg. She keeps speaking. Asta and I can only see them. We can't hear anything. We have to keep up with Fedde. We have to keep ahead of the people behind us with their covered wagons and horses. The road is gravel, but mostly it's muddy from the melted snow. I have a hard time lifting my boots all the way clear of the ruts and sometimes I stumble. Asta tries to talk to the girl.

"Where are you from?"

Nothing.

"Are you also going to Gotenhafen?"

Nothing.

"Where is your mother?"

The baby starts crying and the girl sings to him, so softly we can't hear over the creaking of the wooden cart. I move closer and can hear just enough to recognize the lullaby that Mama used to sing to me until I was much too old, but I still made her when she tucked me into bed at night—"Schlaf, Kindlein, Schlaf."

Sleep, baby, sleep.

Your father guards the sheep.

Your mother shakes a little tree,

And down falls a little dream.

Sleep, baby, sleep.

The father stops the cart. The people behind us, the ones with the horses and wagons, yell at him, yell at all of us. The father pulls the cart far enough over to the side of the road so that they can pass. Mama leads Fedde to the front of the cart and, with the help of the father, lashes him to the handles so he can pull the girl and the baby. We pile our sacks on top of theirs and tie everything in place and then off we go, as if suddenly we have become a family twice the size as we were just moments before.

After awhile, Asta tries again to get the girl to talk, and this time she does.

"I'm Monika," she says. "And the baby is Riki. Papa is Herr Müller."

Asta tells her our names and Monika says hello. We say hello back. It's all very stiff and formal. At first.

"There was a girl in my class named Monika," I tell her. "And I named one of the ducks Monika, too."

Monika seems uncertain how to respond, so Asta explains. "On our grandparents' farm," she says. "There were ducks. Pieta named all of them."

Monika smiles then. "We had ducks, too," she says. "We even brought some duck eggs with us. And one of the ducks."

That makes me excited until I look around for the duck so I can pet it, and then I realize what she means.

Hours later, when we stop for the night, we have a fire for the first time since leaving the farm. Herr Müller has brought plenty of food. Mama cooks a soup with carrots and onions and potatoes and meat that might be the duck. But I don't ask. I'm too hungry. Asta and I eat like little pigs.

Mama and Herr Müller have made a kind of shelter for us under the cart with the horse blankets and a canvas that Herr Müller brought with them. There are other families who are also camped here in this field. They, too, have made shelters and built fires. Some have food. Some come to us and ask if Herr Müller and Mama will share our food with them. But Herr Müller says they can only give a little. It will be a week before we reach Gotenhafen, and we have to be careful with what Herr Müller has brought and only ration out a small amount for each meal. Mama says we are lucky to have found Herr Müller and Monika and Riki. But they are also lucky to have found us. We have Fedde. And Herr Müller has only one leg. The other, the stiff one, isn't a real leg. He explains this to Mama. He laughs when he sees me staring, wide-eyed.

"You want to hear it?" he asks. Asta and Monika, who have been talking already like best friends, stop their conversation and listen, too. Herr Müller taps his shin with his knuckles. It makes a wooden sound, like knocking on a door.

"Papa!" Monika says. "You must stop. Please."

He smiles and shrugs and I stop staring. He is one of the few men on the road who is not very young or very old. Mama says all the rest are in the army.

CHAPTER 19
ASTA

At first I thought Monika would be quiet and shy like Pieta, and I would have to help take care of her, too, now that we have thrown in our lot with the Müllers. That's what Mama says we are doing—throwing in our lot with them. She says they are good people. Farm people like Opa and Oma. And it is to our mutual benefit to join forces. That, too, is how Mama says it. As if we are going into business with the Müllers.

But Monika isn't shy. Just very, very sad. It only takes a little coaxing to get her to talk, to tell me what happened to her mother.

"We were so happy, waiting for Riki to be born," she says as Pieta and I gather closer to her and the small fire. "When the time came, Papa went for the doctor in the village, but everyone had already left. We had to stay until Mama had the baby. But something happened. Papa didn't know what to do. He had to deliver the baby himself. And then he had to bury Mama."

Pieta reaches over to hold my hand. Monika's story is making her sad. I put my arm around her shoulders.

"I wanted to stay at the farm," Monika whispers. She doesn't want her father to hear. It would make him sad again, she says. "I didn't want to leave Mama. Even in the ground. But Papa said we had to go, like everyone else. He said there will be ships on the coast. But I have never been on a ship before. I have only ever been on our farm and in the village. I have never been anywhere else."

I tell her about the Baltic Sea, and about the times when Papa was still with us and took us on outings from Königsberg to play in the sand dunes on the Vistula Strand and splash in the waves when it was summer and the water was warm. I tell her about Mama and Papa bringing us sailing on a small boat in the Vistula Lagoon, in the calm water between the Strand and the shore. I must be making it sound like some sort of paradise, because by the time I'm finished Monika is excited and says she now can't wait to see it.

But of course we're in the dead of winter. And the water will be freezing. And no one will be playing on the sand dunes. And all the people will be the same as us—leaving everything behind in East Prussia, racing to join the evacuation ahead of the Red Army's advance, boarding the promised ships that will be waiting for us in Gotenhafen.

But still, if I have made Monika forget about losing her mother, even for these few moments, that must be a good thing. We sit in warm silence and watch as Mama and Herr Müller store everything away. Mama has already gotten Rikki to sleep. Pieta surprises me by speaking. "In the Romincka Forest, we had to dig caves at night in the snow," she says in her soft voice. "And we buried ourselves inside them to keep warm while we slept."

Monika giggles and says that can't be true. She says that's what the animals do in winter, and are we a family of bears that hibernate? I say yes, because it doesn't even sound real to me anymore, even though it just happened, our nights in the forest. It seems like a dream. Everything does.

"I wish I was a bear," Monika says. "And do you know what I would do? I would hibernate in my snow cave all the way through the winter. All the way through the war. All the way through everything until when I woke up it would be spring."

CHAPTER 20
PIETA

Wagons and wagons and wagons and wagons. Everywhere on the road are wagons. Farm wagons with so many people riding on them. So many people with so many things. Carts like Herr Müller's pulled by people, ponies, goats. And so many people carrying everything they have on their backs. Their children are weighted down. Their pack animals carry loads as Fedde did for us. The road is like a river in that way, and if it stops, if a wagon breaks down or if an old man or an old woman or a child breaks down, some people help and some people curse at them and tell them to move to the side of the road, into the snowy fields or into the muddy fields. And sometimes coming the other way are the Wehrmacht soldiers, only they have motor vehicles, trucks and command cars. They have petrol. They force us off the road as they race to confront the Red Army.

Mama says we are refugees now. I don't know that word so I ask her what it means. We have to steer away from the road to let yet another Wehrmacht unit pass. The faces of the boys in their oversized uniforms make me sad also. It is as if they know that where they are going, they will not come back. I think about how helpless we were in the forest, in the snow, in the circle for the hunt. I think about the guns and the red snow and Asta making me run and run and run.

Mama says, "You understand that because we no longer have a home we can go back to, we have to find some place that will take us in, and we will live there instead?"

I nod. The Wehrmacht trucks splash mud everywhere, but no one seems to notice anymore. And anyway, soon the snow will start up again and the mud will be covered and no one will even remember.

"Where we are going, the village near Hamburg," Mama continues, "that will be our refuge. The shelter in the Romincka Forest was our refuge, but only for a few nights. In Hamburg, we will have a refuge that will be our new home."

Herr Müller is standing nearby but saying nothing. Mama tells us that the Müllers, too, have family near Hamburg. Asta is happy to hear this. I don't know how she and Monika have become such good friends so quickly.

"Our papa is in the army," I tell Monika. I want to be her friend, too. "He is an engineer. He builds bridges for the troops to cross the rivers."

Monika says her papa can't serve because of his leg. But her uncle was in the Wehrmacht. "He was an infantry soldier," she says. "Maybe he marched over your father's bridges."

Her uncle had worked on the farm with her father, Monika tells us, but he died early in the war. It is his wife—Monika's aunt—who lives near Hamburg. She moved back there from East Prussia to be with her family, and soon they will join her, too.

The Wehrmacht convoy passes and Herr Müller calls us to help push the cart back onto the road, and quickly, to keep our place in the long line of refugees. Fedde is struggling. I can see it in the way his head hangs so low again as he plods along in the road. Anything we can do to make it easier for him, like pushing from behind the cart as he climbs up the embankment back onto the road, we must do. We are still a long way from the coast and the ships.

CHAPTER 21
ASTA

We come upon a farm and there is room for everyone—in the farm-house, in the barns, all over. Someone has already built a bonfire when we get there. They have slaughtered chickens and hogs and everywhere families are cooking, everywhere families are smiling. I only hope we aren't too late pulling in that there isn't something, anything, left for us to eat as well. It's been five days and nights on the road with the Müllers, and our food supplies have dwindled. It's funny that already I say "our," but we have become close with Monika's family so quickly that it just seems natural, even though everything we have came from their farm. But Monika and I—we would have been friends no matter what, even if we hadn't been thrown together like this. Of course, she needed someone to confide in, someone who would listen when she talks about her mother, and I have always been a good listener.

Herr Müller orders us to see what we can find on the farm that can still be eaten, and off we go, Monika and I, holding hands. The families who got here first have set themselves up in the empty farmhouse. We can see them through the windows, crowding the kitchen, sitting around the hearth. Others have taken over the barn, making their straw beds for tonight, bedding down their tired horses in stalls. There is an empty stall and still some unclaimed hay, and we run back for Fedde to take him there. Mama reminds us to give him plenty of water. We find a bucket and wait for the longest time at the pump where a line of people are doing the same.

"I'm so thirsty, too," Monika says. "I could drink as much as a horse!" And I laugh and say me too, even though it's not really all that funny. But we're so tired that everything feels a little silly.

Pieta is with us, too. I feel bad because I know I have been ignoring her. But I know I must still be a good big sister to Pieta, so when our turn comes at the pump, I let her drink first. I insist on it. Monika is impatient, but she understands. She has had to take care of Riki since they lost their mother, after all. So she gets it.

We somehow manage to corner a chicken in some bushes just outside the barn. I'm not sure how everyone else here missed it. Mama kills it and plucks it and cuts it up to add to some potatoes and even some carrots we find in the bottom of a bin someone has also overlooked. Herr Müller builds a fire for us in a space we claim in the barn. I know from Opa and Oma's that you never light a fire in a barn—though there was the exception Opa made on Sundays for the church services. It's too dangerous. But since this farm is abandoned and we're all leaving East Prussia, the old rules no longer apply. Soon Mama's stew is cooking in a pot over the open fire. Everybody is thrilled, even little Riki who makes funny little cooing sounds while Mama has him tied to her with a cloth sling. While the stew cooks, Mama puts Monika and me and Pieta in charge to stir— and to guard it from anyone else in the barn who's been eyeing our good fortune. Many of the refugees have nothing, even here. She goes off to see if she can find milk for Rikki.

Herr Müller sets up our sleeping quarters with the horse blankets and the cart, in the same way as if we were outside still in an open field like the nights before. Only here in the barn it's already so much warmer, thanks to all the people crammed inside, and the horses, and the unsafe fires.

That night, Monika and Pieta and I talk about Hamburg. We decide we will have to be friends there, too—all three of us, which makes Pieta especially happy.

"I hope there will still be the ponies," she says. "And the ginger-bread house."

"It sounds like from a fairy tale," Monika says. "But I hope it's not too close to the city. My aunt wrote to us a letter last year and said they had bombing in Hamburg, too, like yours in Königsberg."

"Nothing could be as bad as Königsberg," Pieta says in a quiet voice.

I don't want to talk about the bombing, but it's not the same for Monika. She lost her mother, and that is the most terrible thing that could ever happen. But about the war, she is curious. Even though her family had to flee from their little farm, and even though they lost her uncle, they haven't known the war the way we did in Königsberg.

"They were called white phosphorus bombs," she says. "My aunt told us they burned half of the city. The fire reached so high into the sky that people called it Gomorrah, like in the Bible, when God set fire to the evil city. Only how could Hamburg be evil?"

I can tell Pieta is getting worried, so I try to reassure her. "Opa said the war is coming to an end soon, and it no longer matters who wins because everyone will have to start over. He said everyone is tired of Hitler and ready to move on. So I don't think we have to worry about more bombs.

"And look," I say, still trying to change the subject. "Don't we have this dry barn to sleep in tonight? And didn't we find that chicken, and the potatoes, and the carrots? Soon we will be on a ship. I have seen ships before and you will be amazed, Monika. They are as huge as buildings! And safe. And where they are taking us, if there is still any bombing in Hamburg, they will take us somewhere else. Somewhere safe as well. Somewhere without any more bombing or white phosphorus. I promise. Somewhere without the war."

CHAPTER 22
PIETA

Oh finally! Finally! We are here! And so many people. The long line of people on the road, on all the roads leading to Gotenhafen, have all arrived. Here at the docks there is hardly room for us to stand and Fedde paces nervously. I make sure to be near him all the time—for protection so I am not trampled under all these people—and so that I can stroke his long nose and let him know everything will be all right, because we're here now, finally we're here, and soon we will be on board one of the ships with the other refugees like Mama said.

Herr Müller stands next to the cart, as if he needs to protect it from thieves. He is tall and can look over the heads of most of the people jostling around us in this open square. Asta and Monika sit on top of the cart, wrapped in blankets, holding Riki, and so they are safe from the crowd. A cold wind blows from the direction of the Baltic harbor, though I can't see the water, and this crowd surrounding us is some protection but not enough. I shiver. I hug Fedde again. I blow on my hands to warm them. I press myself against Fedde's side and he lets me lean there. He knows we are friends. He knows I always remind Mama that he needs to be fed, that he needs water, that he needs shelter if there is any to be found. I can tell he doesn't like it here on these cobblestones.

I pull on Mama's sleeve and she bends down to hear me.

"Mama," I whisper. "Can we go somewhere else for Fedde? Somewhere that the ground is softer?"

She looks around, but I already know the answer. "It won't be long," Mama says. "Fedde will be all right here." She points to the other horses to show me he's not alone, but I can tell by the way the other horses keep lifting their hooves and shifting their weight that they don't like it, either.

Mama pats Fedde, too, then tells me she has to go. "We aren't allowed to just board one of the ships," she says. "We have to have tickets. There's a line. Otherwise the ships will be too crowded."

Mama and Herr Müller leave to wait in the ticket line and are soon lost in the crowd.

"Here, Pieta," Asta says from atop the cart. "It's your turn to sit and hold the baby." Monika lays Riki in my lap and wraps us both in the blankets and then lets herself down to join Asta.

"We're going to find food," Asta says, and they hold hands and go off together, leaving me alone for the first time.

I don't have time to think about it, though, or to feel anxious, because Riki starts fussing and squirming. I fumble through the blankets and find a bottle with some milk that has mostly been mixed with water to make it last longer, but the girls have left it exposed and so it's too cold to give Riki. I tuck it under my clothes to warm it, and then softly hum the song that I heard Monika sing that first day when we met them a week before, but that seems so much longer ago.

Hours later, Mama and Herr Müller return with the tickets. Hours after that, Asta and Monika return empty-handed. They say there are too many people who are hungry and thirsty who have descended on the town, and so there's no food anywhere. But no matter.

"We have been assigned to a ship," Mama announces. "Tomorrow we will be allowed to board." She is tired, but I can tell she is trying hard to sound excited for us, to convince us that this is all to be a great adventure. And perhaps it will be. Only who can forget all that has happened? Who can forget Opa and Oma and Rolf and the other soldiers and the farm neighbors who joined us on the hunt? And how can so much time have passed?

Herr Müller speaks next. "We have no choice but to stay here tonight," he says. "We will have to take turns sleeping on the cart. There isn't room to make our camp." Even as he says this, a wave of people presses against us. Herr Müller pushes them away. Another man says angry things to him and for a minute I am afraid they will use their fists on each other, but the wave of people passes on, including the angry man.

Herr Müller says he will try again to find food and drink for us, but Monika says, "Papa, there is nothing. We looked everywhere." He only grunts in response and then he goes. And an hour later he finds us, now in the dark, and he has brown bread, almost an entire loaf. He hands it to Mama and seems proud of himself and Mama smiles and thanks him. He also has a canteen slung over his shoulder that he has managed to fill with water, and he passes that around as Mama breaks apart the bread and give us each our share.

Riki cries, but the bottle is empty and the only thing we have to give him now is the water. He's still too tiny for bread. The long night begins, and as it stretches on, I am colder and colder, the wind whipping hard off the Baltic. Snow starts up and stings my face. Mama shelters the baby with her body. We all share the blankets. We are all miserable. But at least we know that tomorrow we will be on our ship to a new life.

CHAPTER 23
ASTA

Morning arrives, but it's not what we expect. Planes fly over Gotenhafen and everybody screams and tries to run. Only the crowd is too thick. People will be trampled, and so many here are children. Pieta and Monika and I huddle together under the cart with Riki in Monika's lap. My heart is beating so fast that I can hardly breathe. But I am the oldest and I have to stay calm for the others. I hold their hands and we lean in so close to one another that we touch foreheads. Riki is wailing, terrified, and I tell him over and over that it will be okay, as if he can understand me. Mama and Herr Müller press themselves against us from the outside. We feel the shock every time someone crashes into them running past. Fedde whinnies, and Herr Müller strains to hold onto Fedde's rope to keep him from bolting. Soldiers blow their whistles to try to halt the stampede. We cling to one another even more tightly as if the cart is an island and all around us a raging sea. But where are the sirens? Why is there no warning?

The planes fly past. Herr Müller looks up and sees the markings under the wings. "They are German planes," he tells us. "Luftwaffe. There are no bombs."

Once they're gone, the crowd calms itself as if we are all one, as if we all breathe a sigh of relief in unison. But Mama says, "Enough of this. We are too exposed here. We need to get away from the crowd, to somewhere we will be able to find shelter if there is a bombing raid."

Herr Müller nods his agreement, and we pack and start the grinding process of making our way through the packed crowd. Monika and I are behind the cart with Pieta, while Mama, carrying Riki in the cloth sling, holds onto one side of Fedde while Herr Müller guides us all forward from the other.

"Out of the way!" he barks as we squeeze our way through. "Out of the way!"

Men curse back at him, but most grudgingly pull back to allow us through. Pieta clings to my coat sleeve. Monika says, "But aren't we moving in the wrong direction, away from the docks? What will happen when they call our ticket numbers?"

I don't know what to tell her.

We find a crowded park a few streets away from the docks but not as crowded as where we were. There is room to make our camp the way we did on the refugee road. And we wait. There is a delay, but no one tells us anything. One day. Two days. People are angry. There is shouting. Sometimes there are fights. We try to keep to ourselves. Mama and Herr Müller leave us with the baby while they go off for longer and longer excursions, hunting food and water, and milk for Riki, who is always hungry and who Mama says she fears may be malnourished. He fusses less and less. The past few days, he rarely cries. He just lies there with his eyes open. Or he sleeps and sleeps.

Some days we eat. Some days we don't eat. Our stomachs rumble all the time. Mama and Herr Müller find plenty of water, and we drink until we are bloated and can drink no more, until our stomachs ache. And we're still hungry. All around us, people build fires with whatever scraps of wood they can find, but it's not enough to ward off the cold and the fierce wind blowing off the Baltic. We stay huddled together as much as we can.

It is the end of January when we are finally called to board the ship. Mama and Herr Müller gather all the clothes and blankets and tie them into bundles for each of us to carry. Herr Müller fastens the rope to Fedde's halter and I understand what is happening, but I can see from Pieta's lost expression that she hasn't yet figured it out. Not until he starts to lead Fedde away.

Pieta cries out. "NO!"

She flings her arms around Fedde's neck and refuses to let go. She is sobbing, realizing, finally, that Fedde isn't coming with us on the ship. But of course anyone would have known that. The ship isn't Noah's Ark. There are thousands of people, thousands of children waiting.

But Pieta only knows what her heart tells her. I go to her and gently try to pull her away before Mama gets there. Mama has no patience for an outburst like this. Pieta holds tight, and I pull harder while Herr Müller tugs at the rope to force Fedde to follow him. Mama grabs Pieta hard by the shoulders and forces her to let go. Pieta continues sobbing as Herr Müller leads Fedde away, out of the park and down the street until they are out of sight.

"You must stop now," Mama tells Pieta. "You must be a big girl and stop this foolishness. Fedde is only a horse, and he will be a good horse for some other family who needs him. They will take good care of him. And when the war is over, and when the Red Army has gone away, and when we return, who knows? Maybe we'll find Fedde and buy him back. And if not Fedde, then a horse like Fedde."

It's a lie, of course. All of it is a lie. Monika knows it and I know it. We exchange a look that says we both do. We heard Mama and Herr Müller talking while Pieta was asleep. There is a slaughterhouse not far from the docks. They will pay for Fedde. They are buying all the horses that have brought the refugees here to Gotenhafen. The troops who are still doing the fighting must be fed. Everything that can be eaten is now food.

CHAPTER 24
PIETA

Opa once told me that the name Fedde is from the Old German language and it means "peace." I don't know why he told me this. Opa was always telling me things. I wish I could have told him things, but what could I ever tell Opa that he didn't already know? And now it's too late. And now there is no longer Opa. And now there is no longer Fedde. And now no peace, not in my heart or my head.

"There's no time for this," Mama says, pulling me along in the fading late afternoon. Already it's becoming dark and the wind is blowing snow and rain sideways off the Baltic Sea. "We must hurry to the ship. Look, Pieta, see there? No one is standing in a proper queue for boarding. What good were these tickets? What good was waiting our turn? People are swarming all over the docks. See? See? Just up ahead? They say the *Wilhelm Gustloff* can hold two thousand, but there must be five times that number forcing their way on board. Hold on tight to me, girls! Hold onto Herr Müller!"

Mama and Herr Müller are forcing their way toward the ship like everyone else. We all are. People elbow us to get ahead. They shout at us. They shout just to shout, as if that will help them get passage on the ship. Herr Müller is big and strong, and we follow him. He pushes people aside, even women holding babies like Riki. Even children like us. Mama takes out a rope and ties it to our waists so we won't be separated from them, so we won't be lost. I see two girls, twins, I think, and they are lost. They are standing back-to-back, holding on to each other and calling for their mother and their father, but there is no mother or father. We shove by them. Asta reaches out to seize one, to rescue them, to bring them with us, but the girl slaps her hand away.

The bundle Mama gave me to carry is ripped out of my hands and gone before I can see what happens to it. Asta loses hers as well. Monika is the only one who manages to keep her blanket and clothes. Mama says, "No worries about that. In Hamburg there will be more. Now keep up. Keep up!"

I am afraid we will be trampled. The path narrows onto the gang-way, and there are fewer people jammed tightly against us, just ahead and behind. They keep pushing, pushing from behind. Monika falls, but we pull her back to her feet. She is crying. Mama says there's no time for crying. We forge ahead. We keep pressing.

I'm afraid we'll be forced off the gangway and down into the black water between the ship and the dock. It's so steep. The side of the ship rises like a cliff beside us. I can touch it. The gangway sways and bangs into the steel hull. I pull my hand away just in time, but behind me someone doesn't and it smashes their fingers. They shriek. We keep going. We keep going. We keep going. Until finally we are on the ship, herded onto the deck.

The crew in their sailor's uniforms have poles they use to prod people, to force them through doors that will take them somewhere inside the *Wilhelm Gustloff,* maybe down below the deck. Or maybe higher, to heated cabins and staterooms. I see stairs just beyond the doorway. I start to follow, eager to finally be warm, but the sailors form a line in front of us and block the way.

"No more room," one shouts. "All others must remain on deck."

People keep pouring up the gangway and onto the ship, pressing against us, trying to force their way inside, but the sailors won't budge. Mama pulls us away and leads us to outside stairs. We climb after her and keep climbing until we're on the highest deck on the *Wilhelm Gustloff,* huddled under a long row of lifeboats that hang over our heads on thick ropes tied to the side of the ship. Monika and Asta and I sit in a circle again with the baby in the middle. Mama and Herr Müller protect us from the surging crowd that follows us here.

Things calm down eventually, after the sailors raise the

gangplank. Mama takes Riki. She feels his face, then unwraps the blankets and feels his pink skin. He is sweating, despite the cold.

"Rikki has a fever," she says to Herr Müller. "He cannot be here on the deck, exposed to the freezing wind and rain."

Suddenly I'm aware of it, too, how cold and wet and windy it is. In the rush of boarding, in the madness, I didn't feel it, but now that we're here, I do. Asta is shivering, too. And Monika.

"We should be inside then," Herr Müller says, taking Riki.

"There are too many of us," Mama says. "We'll stay here. You go with Riki and Monika. They'll let you in with a baby who is sick."

Herr Müller tries to argue, but Mama insists they will have a better chance of convincing the sailors to let Rikki inside where it's warm, where they will be out of the weather.

Herr Müller finally agrees.

Asta and Monika hug and then Herr Müller, Rikki, and Monika disappear into the crowd. There are horns and whistles and so much more shouting. I press my hands over my ears. Mama has found a canvas that she wraps around us, our backs pressed against the rail as the ship pulls out of the Gotenhafen port. The lifeboats hanging over our heads give us some shelter, and we are so high up here on the highest deck that the waves can't reach us, though they rock the ship from side to side, and up and down.

People around us who try to stand are knocked down and have to crawl their way back to their families. Anything not held down or tied down is blown overboard. Mama has her arms around us and pulls us tightly against her. It will be a long trip, she warns us. Already I feel seasick and frozen. Below deck must be so much warmer where Herr Müller and Monika and Riki are. Out of the biting wind and the bitter, bitter cold, and the stinging rain and snow. I crane my neck to look behind us, but already Gotenhafen has vanished into the ocean fog.

CHAPTER 25
ASTA

A few hours out to sea and my teeth won't stop chattering, but I can't squeeze myself any closer to Mama to get warm. Poor Pieta has fallen asleep with her head in Mama's lap. Everyone around us is huddled together in the same way, buried as much as they can be buried under blankets and stolen canvas pulled free from the lifeboats. And still it's not enough to escape the awful cold.

Mostly I hear the shrieking of the wind and the rough waves below crashing against the sides of the ship. But there's something else and it takes me a little while before I realize it's Mama, and she's singing. I can hardly believe it—for her to be singing now, here, and yet she is. I strain to hear the song, but it's as if the wind steals the words as soon as they escape her lips.

I want to ask her what song it is, and I struggle to sit up, but before I can there is an explosion, and the world goes silent for a moment.

My heart is suddenly in my throat. Then, out of nowhere, there's another explosion, and then another. The ship is lifted out of the water, slammed back down. We are thrown against the rail as the ship rocks hard from side to side with noise so loud I don't know where it's coming from. An old man sitting near us is flung over the side and vanishes. All around us there is screaming. Mama squeezes my arm so hard it hurts. She grabs Pieta. I'm one of the ones screaming, frightened, panicked. Mama tells me, "Stop! Stop!"

Horns, sirens, whistles blast from everywhere. People are staggering up the ladders, streaming out of the hatches from the hidden decks below. Flames erupt around us. Sailors appear above us and immediately begin lowering the lifeboats. I am clinging to the rail, crushed against it by the swarm of desperate passengers. One of the lifeboats sways next to us, but before we can climb in, we are overwhelmed with people fighting their way past us to board. Sailors are struggling to stop them, but they're outnumbered, shoved to the side, ignored.

Mama lifts Pieta and throws her in the boat. She lands on top of others, a jumble of people. Mama seizes me, but I won't let her pick me up.

"NO!" I yell, afraid she won't come, too.

A flood of others follow Pieta into the lifeboat, which is already overfull, and Mama manages to shove me in after them, just as the ship lurches farther onto its side. Mama is still on the deck while the lifeboats are dangling loose over the water. The sailors start cranking the winches furiously to lower them. I am reaching for Mama, but already it's too late, already she's receding as we drop lower, closer and closer to the rough sea. I can see now that the whole ship is on fire. People are jumping over the sides and past us into the water, some in life jackets, some without.

Another lifeboat breaks loose and plummets past us and slams into the water below. Everyone on board is thrown into the water. People who have fallen in, or jumped, swim frantically over to other boats to pull themselves in. Our lifeboat stops halfway down. Something has jammed. A boy near me pulls out a hunting knife. He slashes at a jammed cable as everyone else clings the sides. The heavy rope snaps and we drop like the other boat, hard into the sea. I land on top of other passengers. People keep screaming, many of them in pain. A wave crashes over us. We are stunned. And soaked. But floating. I yell, "Pieta, Pieta, Pieta," and there's a hand on my arm and it's her. She's caught beneath a woman who isn't moving. Others help me roll the woman off Pieta and my little sister throws herself into my arms and I'm holding her and we're both crying. They lift the woman and dump her body into the water to make room for others trying to claw their way on. People are dragged on board. Someone has an oar and is trying to paddle, to get us away from the ship, which is listing more and more onto one side, threatening to roll over on top of us. Panicked, I scan the crowd hanging onto the deck rails high above but don't see Mama anywhere. I see more bodies dropping. So many dropping. The flames are rising higher and higher and higher on the ship. Two men now have oars and are using them not to help us escape the listing ship but to push people away. We are so many on the lifeboat that I'm afraid we will tip over. Everyone is afraid. People keep grabbing the sides and try to pull themselves onboard, but there's no room, but how can we not save them? The men with the oars swing them at the drowning people, hitting their hands, forcing them to let go, driving them back into the freezing water. Waves wash over them. They disappear. Or they float in their life preservers. Begging and begging. Until they stop begging and stop screaming and stop crying. Until they lie motionless. Face down. But the fighting continues because there's still not enough room. We are wedged in so tightly that it's hard to breathe. People moan beneath us but can't free themselves. Pieta and I cling tightly to each other and try to make ourselves smaller so there might be more room. The men with the oars are now paddling furiously to get us away from the sinking ship. The *Wilhelm Gustloff* rolls all the way over onto its side and then goes under, surely taking thousands down with it. I pray that Mama has found a way to survive, that she's made her way to another lifeboat, that when morning comes she will find us and she will be alive and she will tell us what we're supposed to do.

CHAPTER 26
PIETA

The bright orange lifejackets are all around us on the open sea. Asta tells me not to look. It is too terrible. I look anyway. I can't see the faces. All through the night, men have tried to paddle us away from them, away from the faces we can still see, and the voices, begging, faintly begging, away from the ship that isn't anymore. The only face I want to see besides Asta's is Mama's. The only voice I want to hear is hers.

I ask Asta over and over, "Where's Mama? Why isn't she here?" She says Mama must be on another boat and we will see her soon. I want to believe her, but I don't believe her, but I *have* to believe her.

I try to count the lifejackets, but it's like counting stars in the sky. And my eyelashes freeze if I look too long. I do it to make myself stop thinking about Mama. The lifejackets remind me of the ducks on Opa and Oma's pond, and the nursery song, *All my ducklings, swimming on the lake, swimming on the lake. Heads in the water, little tails up in the air.* Asta tells me I must bury myself in between the others on the lifeboat. Every time we have to let someone go—someone whose eyes have stopped seeing—we take off their coat first, then anything else warm. A hat. A muffler. Mittens. Asta makes sure I have layers of wool to protect me from the wind and sleet, and from the waves sloshing over the boat.

The women who can take over from the men at the oars. But so many are injured and bleeding, or burned, or refuse to give up the children they are holding, children whose eyes have also stopped seeing. One of the women wearing a uniform paddles so hard that we turn the wrong way and the men tell her to ease up. But how do they even know? It's morning but that only means the dark gray of night is a lighter gray with fog as thick as broth. The uniformed woman curses the captain of the *Wilhelm Gustloff* and the navigation lights. The lights, the lights, the lights, the stupid, stupid lights. She says it must have been a submarine. A Soviet submarine that found us and targeted us and torpedoed us not once, not twice, but three times. Three times!

I press my mittens over my ears and try to block out her voice. I sing to myself, "Schlaf, Kindlein, Schlaf" over and over until she finally, finally stops.

• • • • • • • • • • •

I know Mama is gone. Asta tells me again and again that Mama is on another lifeboat and she will find us somehow. Every time she brings it up, the story changes about when and where we'll see Mama again. But I saw already. I saw Mama at the rail, reaching for Asta's hand. I saw the people jumping and falling into the water. I saw the ship roll over on its side. I saw the *Wilhelm Gustloff* disappear into the Baltic Sea. I saw the whirlpool that followed, pulling everyone still too close down with it. I saw the undrowned trying to climb into the lifeboats, but the boats were too full and threatened to tip over. I saw the men with their oars pushing the undrowned away, even children. I saw a lifeboat so crowded and so low in the water that when a wave struck, it floundered and sank and the people sank with it. Except for the ones in lifejackets who kept floating face down, the ones who still surround us now as morning has broken.

I was the one who taught Mama that song when I was four: *All my ducklings, swimming on the lake, swimming on the lake. Heads in the water, little tails up in the air.* I thought I was the one who taught her, anyway. I know now that she was just pretending. She must have known it all along.

CHAPTER 27
ASTA

They come from the shore. Men in rescue boats, summoned from a village near Gotenhafen by the *Wilhelm Gustloff* captain's last radio appeal for help. They tell us we're safe now, that the Soviet submarines will stay farther out to sea in deep water. They tie a rope to our lifeboat and give us blankets and water and bread and tow us in through a field of floating mines. I hold my breath every time we sweep close by one, anchored just below the surface. But the men know their way. They are grim. We see other boats lifting bodies from the sea, hauling them in by their lifejackets, which have kept them afloat but didn't save any of them in the freezing water. Even some we rescued died from exposure on the way in. Some are still in the lifeboat with us as we're towed into protected water bounded by an unfinished pier. We are at the mouth of a river that flows into the Baltic. The village is built up on the banks of both sides. I smell wood fires and coal fires from morning stoves. But I also still smell the ship, the foul stench of burning oil and melting steel. And every time I close my eyes I see Mama, reaching for me, shouting to me, then gone. I think I shouldn't close my eyes, then. I should keep them open until I find her, until she returns to us, until all this horror goes away.

When we reach the dock, I can't stand. My legs won't hold me. Pieta, who I have sheltered all these hours with my body, takes my hand and tries to help me up, but my legs still don't work. I've been sitting in the cramped space on the lifeboat for too long. Men climb on board. They move the lifeless bodies to the center of the boat and help everyone else off. They lift me onto the dock. I am the last. Even Pieta is able to climb there. She waits for me. We stumble together on our frozen legs behind the feeble line of survivors up the path and into a small, weathered church where women offer us dry blankets and mugs of hot cider and plates of food. We sit on a pew and try to eat and try to drink, but it's so warm and we're so tired that we set our food and drink aside and curl up on the pew and both of us are soon dead asleep.

· · · · · · · · · · ·

Bodies are lined up outside when we wake, and my first thought again is Mama. How could I have fallen asleep? I am angry with myself. Who has been checking to see if one of them might be her? And if one of them is, who has thought to check her pulse, her heart, her breath to see if there has been a mistake, and she is alive? I should find out before Pieta does so I can still save Mama. Or so I can prepare Pieta. Or lie to her.

I climb off the pew, but my wobbly legs still aren't working right and I sag into the aisle. Helpful people rush to me, but I push them away. I struggle to stand on my own, holding the back of one of the pews. Pieta lifts her head and looks, but her eyes aren't focused and she lies back down. I make my way through the door and into the churchyard. It's freezing, the icy wind still blowing hard off the Baltic.

I don't have my jacket, only a blanket over my shoulders. I cover my head with it, like a hood, and tramp through the snow to look at the faces, to look for Mama. Most of them are children. I don't have to spend any time looking at them. I don't want to see them. One of them could be Monika, or Riki, but I don't want to know. I only want to know about Mama. I quicken my pace. The line goes on and on, past the church grounds and into the cemetery, bodies laid on top of graves. Every time a boat pulls into the cove they bring more. And every time, none of them is Mama, and every time my heart sinks. I look back at the church and Pieta is there, watching me. She waves. I gesture for her to go inside. She doesn't even have a blanket. A woman tries to coax her back into the church, but she refuses to go. She won't take her eyes off me. Every time I look, she's still there. She's not looking for Mama. She's only looking out for me. So finally

I give up. I will never find Mama. Or Herr Müller. Or Monika. Or Riki. There are thousands who must have gone down with the *Wilhelm Gustloff*, thousands lost to the Soviet torpedoes and the black waters of the Baltic. As many as they have pulled from the water and brought to this place, these are only a few of the dead.

For hours afterward, Pieta and I hold each other and sob. Neither of us can speak. I can't think of anything to say to comfort her. We slip off the pew and onto the floor and still we cling to each other in our grief. People come to help us back up and I tell them to go away, to leave us alone. Pieta says nothing. She buries her face against me and I wrap us in the blanket they've given us and I don't know what to do.

• • • • • • • • • • •

Finally, when it's night, we climb back onto our pew. We eat the remnants of food on our plates, though it's been sitting all day. We sit in silence, leaning against each other, empty, still not able to speak. Every time the church door opens, I look. And every time I see the face of someone else who has lost everyone and everything.

We make room on the pew as the church becomes more and more crowded. More lifeboats have been found. More survivors. But not so many that the church is ever full. We sleep again. Pieta makes small noises that wake me. I put my arm around her and hold her to me. She is all I have left, and I am all she has now, too. I will never, ever, ever let go of her. I can't. If I were to be separated from Pieta, I don't know what would become of her. She couldn't survive on her own. And if I were to ever lose her, I don't know what would become of me, either. I can't imagine a life without her. I can't imagine a life alone.

And so we stay like this, together. Through the day and the night. Through most of the next day—sleeping, eating what we're given, bowing our heads when there are prayers, keeping silent when there are hymns, excusing ourselves and holding hands when we have to visit the outhouse. And when a wagon arrives to take us back to Gotenhafen—the dozens of us who are now orphans—we bundle ourselves under blankets together. The boy with the hunting knife, the one who cut us free from the *Wilhelm Gustloff* a lifetime ago, sits beside us. He was so brave then to do what he did. But now he can't stop crying. I ask him if he has also lost his mother, but he can only shake his head, and after awhile we let him in under the blankets, too.

CHAPTER 28
PIETA

The boy has attached himself to us like a barnacle on a boat. I don't know how I thought of that, but I did. And I call him that, too. The Barnacle. I whisper it to Asta. She is surprised, I know, that I have found my whisper voice again. I am surprised, too. Then she corrects me. "His name is Gerhard." And now I think, *Gerhard the Barnacle*, but I don't say it out loud, not even a whisper. Because Asta reminds me that he has lost his mother and his whole family, but so what? We have lost our mother and our whole family, too. Except for someone, I forget who, in Hamburg. Already I am forgetting things. I'm already forgetting Oma and Opa, their voices. Even their faces I can only see now as though they are outside and I am inside and the window is dirty and streaked with rain.

We have built a fort for ourselves in a corner of the big gymnasium where they have brought all the orphans. Me and Asta and

Gerhard the Barnacle. He fiddles with his knife all the time, unless one of the matrons comes by, in which case he hides it until they are past. He's not like Rolf back on Opa and Oma's farm—he doesn't carve anything. Maybe if he had some wood he might carve something, but I don't think so. The Barnacle's knife is too big for whittling.

We sit, not knowing what else to do. There is nothing else to do. We wait. Sometimes there is news. Or rumors. It's impossible to tell the difference. The matrons talk among themselves. They say there were ten thousand on board the *Wilhelm Gustloff* and five thousand were children and only one thousand survived.

One of the matrons, a small woman who stands near us, realizes we have overheard their conversation.

"You children," she says, with sad eyes. "You must know you are the lucky ones. You must remember to thank God for your salvation."

We nod and say, "Yes, Fräulein, yes, of course," but as soon as she leaves, Asta fumes.

"I don't think we are lucky at all," she says. "Because we lost Mama. And Monika and Riki and Herr Müller. And Gerhard also lost his family."

Gerhard the Barnacle nods but doesn't say anything.

Asta is so angry that she kicks a plate of food, sending a potato flying across the room. It lands in a boy's lap and he picks it up, looks at it, glances around to see where it might have come from, and then eats it.

The Barnacle and I giggle, but not Asta. "It's not funny," she snaps. "Don't laugh. Nothing is funny anymore."

The boy who ate the potato licks his fingers and smiles and looks around for more potatoes falling from the sky. The Barnacle and I laugh harder.

But Asta is right. Soon we hear that another ship has been sunk by the submarines in the Baltic and five thousand more, most of them soldiers this time, have been lost.

When they let us outside the gymnasium to exercise, we stand around with the others and shiver and stamp our feet in the snow. The Barnacle asks an older boy why they don't let us ride on trains or in trucks to Germany.

The older boy has a bandage covering one of his eyes and the side of his face. His arm is in a sling. He was on the *Wilhelm Gustloff*, too. He cups his good ear so the Barnacle can repeat what he asked, then he shakes his head.

"The partisans in Poland have stopped all the trains from East Prussia," the older boy says. "They are stopping all cars and trucks. They won't let any Germans through."

"What about our army—" the Barnacle starts, but the boy cuts him off.

"The Wehrmacht is retreating from Poland," he says. "Don't you know this? Now for Germans to go through Poland is to meet death. There are only the ships from Gotenhafen. And those can mean death, too."

The Barnacle turns away. He is quiet for a long time.

When he finally speaks, it's to Asta and me. "I will run away before I let them put me on another ship."

But what else is there for us? We see ship after ship, boat after boat, leaving the harbor for the evacuation.

"Some of them must get through," I whisper to Asta. But I think she listens more to the Barnacle, who has now fastened himself closer to her because it is in her ear that he speaks, and it is she who nods in a way she doesn't when I whisper my thoughts. She pats me on the shoulder. She even pats me on the head sometimes, as if I am a little child and she is the mother.

Until one day we are told there will be passage for us on the next ship leaving Gotenhafen, and we must be ready to go to the docks in the morning. Only that night, late that night, after we have eaten the watery stew, black bread, and moldy apples that they serve us, and after I have fallen asleep on my blanket bed that is all the cushion on this hard gymnasium floor, Asta wakes me, shaking me gently, and then harder. She puts a hand over my mouth when I start to cry out, not knowing what's going on. She says, "Come now, Pieta. We're leaving. Grab everything."

I sit up. *Everything?* But we don't have anything except the blankets we've been given, and our clothes, and the clothes of the dead that were taken from them and handed to us on the lifeboat. There is nothing else.

But there is. Gerhard the Barnacle has stolen more blankets and food—more black bread and apples. And a sausage from somewhere! He has other things he ties up in a sack and throws over his shoulder. Asta jams a hat on my head that falls all the way down over my ears. We follow the Barnacle as he crawls around the sleepers to a side door that screeches when he drags it open. We hold still for one minute, two minutes, but no matrons come. Perhaps they are asleep as well. Soon we are outside in the snow in the dead of night, and Gerhard says, "This way," and we follow him, though I am surprised that Asta is willing and that she trusts him to know what he's doing and where he's going and where he's leading us.

I ask her but she shushes me. I keep asking her, until she turns in the middle of a silent street and says, "We are going back to Königsberg."

CHAPTER 29
ASTA

The road to Danzig, the next city over, is still streaming with refugees, all of them heading in the opposite direction of us. Just one week ago, we were among those refugees. I can't help but think about the Müllers now, about Monika and how quickly we became friends, and how quickly I lost my friend. How suddenly you can lose everyone and everything.

But I can't dwell on that now. Gerhard wants to steal a wagon and a pony, but I say no to that. We have been walking for only a few hours, out of Gotenhafen and following the highway south. Gerhard says he has seen a map, and the shortest route for us is to Danzig, and from there we simply follow the Vistula Spit, that long, narrow strand of beach and dunes and stands of pine that protects the Vistula Lagoon from Danzig Bay and the rough waters of the Baltic Sea. He says the crossing will take us a week, maybe two weeks. The Vistula Lagoon is where Papa and Mama took us boating so many years ago before the war. But that was at the far eastern end. The end that is near home, if there is enough left of Königsberg to call it that again.

"Come," Gerhard says to me. "See there? A wagon. Abandoned already." And sure enough, on the side of the highway are several wagons and carts, shoved off the road and left for anyone who might want them.

"We should stop here for the night," I say. "We can sleep under one of the wagons. And tomorrow, maybe we will find a pony, too. But not one that we steal."

I look at Pieta and she is yawning and shivering. I take her hand, and we make our way to the abandoned wagons. Fires are burning at camp sites all around us. Gerhard says we should build a fire, too, and he goes to work prying and kicking loose boards from one of the carts to use as fuel. He knows what he's doing and has thought to bring matches, and before long he has a blaze going next to one of the wagons. Instead of climbing under it to sleep, I make a tent between the seats and crawl in with a tired Pieta. Gerhard sits for awhile by his fire, disappointed that we don't want to stay up with him. In the morning, he is under the blankets with us, though, and the fire has gone out. I can see why Pieta calls him the Barnacle. I hear him when he crawls in under the covers and he cries himself to sleep, there in the dark where he thinks no one can see or hear. He's done it every night since the ship went down. I realize that I haven't cried since that afternoon with Pieta. I have become afraid, I think, that if I let myself start again, I may never stop.

Gerhard builds another fire in the morning from the ashes. We huddle close around it, still under our blankets. A heavy fog rolls in from the Baltic Sea and we have to wait for it to lift before we continue our journey.

Gerhard tells us his plan. "First we find a pony."

Pieta rolls her eyes. "You already said that," she says in her quiet voice.

He huffs. "Well, we can't pull the cart ourselves, you know."

"What after that?" I ask, before Pieta can say anything more. They don't seem to like each other very much.

"Supplies," Gerhard says. "In Danzig, we gather what we can find for crossing the Vistula Spit. It will take a long time to reach Königsberg on foot."

"I thought we were going to ride on the cart," Pieta says. "With the pony."

"Not all of us at once," he responds. "And anyway, when we get to Königsberg, we will have to find more supplies, because we will be there only a short time."

"Mama said there is a records office," I say. "For the army. We should find it and see if we can learn where Papa is. To send a message and let him know what happened to Mama. Maybe they'll bring him back to be with us."

"Yes," Gerhard says. "Okay. That also. But then we go to my aunt and uncle's farm. They refused to leave. It is next to the Memel Forest, east of the city, near the Memel River. On the other side of the river is Lithuania."

"But what if the Red Army goes there, too?" I ask, and Pieta nods. "What then?"

"My uncle knows the Memel Forest, and we can hide there with them until the Red Army leaves. Then they will return to the farm. It is a long way from any village. It will be safe there."

"You're sure of this?" I ask. "And how do you know the way?"

He hesitates. "I stayed there with them in the summers," he says, which isn't really an answer.

• • • • • • • • • • •

The streets of Danzig are almost empty, and we wander through them looking for food, for anything that might be useful for our trek across the Vistula Spit. Gerhard tries doors to see if they have been left unlocked. A few open, but there are people inside and they shout at us.

At one, we think we are lucky. The door opens and no one is home. We find food in the kitchen. So much food! A sack of potatoes. One with onions. Sausages hanging from a rack on the ceiling. A pitcher of milk that has turned only a little sour. When I find a fresh loaf of bread, I stop exclaiming about all the bounty we have found. Gerhard and Pieta stop, too. Because why would this all still be here?

But too late. A man steps out of a closet. He has a gun. We stumble away, frightened, unable to speak. Behind him are children. He starts to say something and then stops. Maybe because we are children, too. He seems as surprised to see us as we are to see him.

He regains his voice. He lowers the gun. "Put everything back," he says, shaking his head. "We don't have enough for you."

"Please," Pieta says. "We are hungry."

I'm surprised again—this time to hear her be the one to speak.

A woman steps out of the closet with the children. They still seem frightened. They are very small. I apologize. "We didn't think anyone was here," I say. "We were looking for food for our journey."

"We don't have enough to share," the man says again. The woman takes the potatoes and onions from my hands. I had forgotten I was even holding them. Gerhard lays the sausages down on the table. Pieta is still holding the loaf of black bread.

We back out of the kitchen, and then out of the house. Pieta keeps the bread. No one says anything. They lock the door behind us, and we turn and run.

Later, we walk past the famous square where there is supposed to be a fountain with a sculpture of the ocean god Neptune holding his trident and riding a seahorse. We saw a picture of it once in school. But it was damaged in one of the Allied bombing raids and they moved it to a secret town. All around us are the wrecks of other buildings. Not as terrible as Königsberg, but what could ever be?

We press on, wagon-less, pony-less. More and more people, refugees, keep passing us on their way to Gotenhafen. I want to shout at them, to warn them, but warn them what? That our ship was sunk by Soviet torpedoes? That they should turn back and go home? But instead, some of them shout at us: "Come!" they say. "You're going the wrong way! The Red Army is coming! We must evacuate while we can."

But if there is death in either direction—in both directions—how do you choose?

Pieta keeps asking me why we are returning, as if Gerhard hasn't already explained his plan.

"Will the records office still be there after the bombing?" she asks. "And why hasn't Papa already come home? Why didn't he come to find us at Opa and Oma's? And what if the Barnacle's aunt and uncle are gone, too?"

So many questions. But every time I start to change my mind, every time I find myself wanting to reassure Pieta, to give in and tell her that we will turn around and go back to Gotenhafen, that we will try again on another ship, a wave of fear washes over me and I feel as though I'm already drowning.

Better to brave the journey across the Vistula Spit. Better to hope that Königsberg is still standing, and that Gerhard's aunt and uncle have survived in the Memel Forest and can take us in. Better to pray that someday Papa will come back to East Prussia and find us.

CHAPTER 30
PIETA

Asta tells me again that we have been here before, on the Vistula Spit, but I don't believe her. I don't remember. "Not here *exactly*," she says. "But at the other end. Papa and Mama took us. You were little. We both were. It was before the war."

But I still don't remember. And why would they bring us to this frozen place where the wind blows so hard off the Baltic Sea that it hurts? There are even patches of ice in the sand that make us slip and fall. The line of people we meet, the refugees, they are all as gray as the waves and the sky.

Asta says, "Not in the winter like now. It was summer then. We played in the water. We built sandcastles."

I shake my head. Gerhard the Barnacle, who has been listening, grunts. He carries so much on his back that he can't straighten his legs as he walks. Asta and I carry as much as we can—water and food and stolen clothes and borrowed blankets—but nothing like the Barnacle.

It is Asta, not the Barnacle, who convinces the ferryman to take us across the mouth of the Vistula River, which interrupts the Vistula Spit a day away from Danzig. The Barnacle argues with the man. He puffs out his chest and says that as proud Germans who refuse to run from the enemy, we deserve free passage, and so what if we have no money?

The ferryman looks down at the Barnacle and laughs.

This is when Asta steps in. "We are trying to join our parents," she says. "Please. If we can only get across, we'll be able to find them on the other side." She looks at Gerhard the Barnacle and rolls her eyes for the ferryman to see. "My brother," she says. "He can be so silly sometimes."

The ferryman lets us board. Hardly anyone is crossing here to go east. Across the river we can see a crowd of refugees waiting for the western crossing so they can continue the trek to Gotenhafen and what they think will be their rescue. I still wish we were going with them. I still wish we had never left. I don't want to return to Königsberg. I don't ever want to go there again.

• • • • • • • • • • •

Soon we are past the river, past the crowd, past the last village. Gerhard the Barnacle says that from here we only have to follow the curving shoreline for as long as it takes, to the end of the Spit, the end of the

Vistula Lagoon. And so all the rest of the day we walk and we walk. We make room for the line of refugees going the other way with their children and their animals and their carts. The Barnacle is jealous and says so every time we see a horse or a donkey or even a dog, all of them carrying heavy bundles tied onto their backs. "Why won't you let me steal one?" he says to Asta.

They are already sounding like a squabbling brother and sister.

"Because someone might arrest you," Asta says.

The Barnacle scoffs. "No one is being arrested. Not for anything. Not anymore."

"Then they might shoot you," Asta says. "Like that man in the house in Danzig."

The Barnacle stops walking. He drops his heavy sack and then drops himself into the wet sand. The sleet has stopped, but it is still freezing, and even though I want to rest I don't want to be cold. As long as we are moving, I'm not so cold. And I'm worried about where we'll sleep tonight. There's not even enough snow on the Vistula Spit to dig a snow cave the way Mama did in the Romincka Forest. But perhaps one of the refugee families will let us stay with them in a tent or under a wagon or a cart. Perhaps they'll convince Asta to change her mind about returning to Königsberg.

"Come, Gerhard," Asta says. "There's no shelter here. We should climb over the dunes if we're going to stop, to be out of this freezing wind."

The Barnacle shakes himself like one of Opa's dogs. He rolls over onto his hands and knees and pushes himself onto his feet. He struggles to lift the sack over his shoulder and then stumbles on. We follow. Asta has told me that the Barnacle is from Königsberg the same as us, only a different part of the city, a neighborhood that escaped the bombing. But no one has escaped the war.

A few hours later, Asta and Gerhard the Barnacle decide we should cross the dunes after all. It's hard walking through sand, even frozen sand, and the icy wind is blowing harder and harder. I can't feel my hands or my feet or my face. There are chunks of ice on the shore. There is protection behind the dunes, and even a narrow path under sheltering pines where we walk in single file until the darkness descends and we have to stop for the night. This time when the Barnacle builds his fire and buries potatoes to cook under the coals, Asta and I stay as close as we can without being burned.

CHAPTER 31
ASTA

There are sounds in the morning, strange sounds, the sounds of engines, softer, then louder, then softer again. A high-pitched whining, punctuated by sharp blasts. Airplanes. Machine guns. The ground shakes from explosions. We wake up screaming, clutching one another. It is only just light out, but the wrong kind of light. Gray. Misty. Pieta calls my name, though she is next to me inside our makeshift shelter, a canvas tied to two pines hidden in the dunes. Gerhard, who always tries to be so brave, is crying and calling for someone, too. His mother. He is confused. We are all just kids and we are frightened and there's no one who will come.

But I am the oldest. I have to do something. I shake myself loose from the two of them, who are holding me so tightly that I have to peel off their fingers one by one. "Wait here," I tell them. Pieta begs me not to leave her. Gerhard is trembling. He covers his ears.

I climb to the top of the dune that has been our protection from the sharp, icy Baltic wind all through the night and am shocked and terrified by what I see below: planes with red stars on the undersides of their wings—Soviet planes—diving out of the gray sky, flashes of fire erupting from their twin guns, bullets raking a caravan of refugees helpless and exposed on the beach. Craters, and bodies, where bombs have exploded. Bodies thrown into the rough surf. Horses and wagons lying on their sides. Tents shredded and flapping in the morning gale. The planes change their targets, following the fleeing survivors who have dropped everything and are racing for cover, right toward us. I don't want to see any more, but I can't look away. I'm frozen, overwhelmed by the horror. But only for a moment—

I roll down the dune, my ears ringing from the explosions, my heart pounding, and shout to Gerhard and Pieta that we have to leave. We grab everything we can, but we're already overrun by the mob. They continue past us, out onto the frozen lagoon where they are just as exposed as before on the beach. The planes follow them there. We cower under the canvas, as if it can make us invisible. And maybe it does. It has pulled loose from the trees and is collapsed over top of us. The planes sweep past several more times, their guns chewing up the snow and ice that blanket the Vistula Lagoon. And then they leave. Out of ammunition. Out of petrol. Out of targets. Who can say?

I hold Pieta and promise her the planes are gone and we're safe now, trying to convince myself as well. Gerhard rouses himself, wipes his eyes, looks around as if he's embarrassed that someone might have seen him so frightened. The wind and snow grow fierce, as if summoned by the assault. It has grown so cold and so awful that I think we might die here if we lie down and sleep. It wouldn't take the Soviet planes refueling and rearming their guns. It would only take giving up.

The survivors return to their wagons, half as many as before. The kids I think are too frozen to cry. The parents lash most of the remaining horses to most of the remaining wagons and they continue on. They don't have anywhere to bury their dead. Gerhard checks the sky again to make sure it is still empty of Soviet planes, then he goes out on the beach and corrals one of the horses that's been left behind. He feeds it whatever he can find, then backs it up to an abandoned wagon and fits it with the harness. We scavenge from among the fallen: food, water, mittens, scarves, sweaters, coats, blankets, knit hats and hoods, then climb onto the wagon.

Pieta finds a doll and clutches it tightly to her. She sits in the back, shell-shocked, cradling her baby. Gerhard snaps the reins and we go. Trying, and failing, to leave behind the nightmare of what we just saw.

· · · · · · · · · ·

At first we stay on the Vistula Spit, but we're scanning the sky for planes the whole time and making slow headway along the beach where the wind is so relentless and fierce and the sand slows us down. Gerhard has the idea that we will make better time traveling on the frozen lagoon, so the next time there's a break in the dunes, we make our way through.

The farther we travel to the east, the more people we meet on the ice—all of them going west, toward Gotenhafen. Days and days go by in this way. Kilometer after kilometer, horror after horror. We see others—bodies—who have fallen and been unable to get up. Bodies left because they could no longer keep up and their friends or loved ones could no longer wait. Bodies of people and animals floating face down in the lagoon where the ice broke and their wagons fell through and they froze to death or they drowned. And every time we see an abandoned cart or wagon, we search it for more blankets, more clothes, any food of any kind. I can't let myself think about the people who once had these things. It would be too sad, too awful. I can only think about our survival.

Twice more over the days that follow—days when the temperature must be well below freezing—the planes return and terrorize the procession of refugees. We don't stop. We can't. Our horse collapses. Worn out, starving, ill. We find another. I don't know how we stay alive. We beg for food. Most people ignore us. Or threaten us if we get too close to their wagons. But some are kind.

One night we share a shelter with an elderly couple. They are riding in a small cart filled with straw and covered by canvas. We have picked up a discarded metal washtub, and Gerhard starts a fire inside with fistfuls of the old people's straw and splintered side boards off a wrecked wagon nearby.

The old woman pulls out pots and pans. She melts snow, balancing a pot on the edge of the washtub. My stomach rumbles as I watch her cut up carrots and onions and potatoes and greens and dump them all in. She even adds a pinch of salt from a small jar she takes out of her coat pocket.

"When was the last time you had a hot meal?" she asks us.

I'm not sure I can remember. Pieta doesn't speak. She's too busy rocking her doll. Gerhard says, "The shelter. In Gotenhafen."

"You are coming from there already?" the old man asks. "Why not on one of the ships? We are traveling to find passage on one of the ships. To Germany. Everyone is going there."

"We were already on a ship," I tell them, though I don't look up. I'm too busy myself—staring at the boiling water and the dancing vegetables. I hold my frozen hands over the rising steam.

"And your parents?" says the old woman.

"Our mother was also on the ship," I tell her. From her expression, I know I don't have to explain any more. But I do. Some. "Gerhard's family was also on the ship. Now it is just the three of us. We are going back to Königsberg. Then to Gerhard's farm in the Memel Forest."

"My aunt and uncle's farm," Gerhard corrects me.

The soup will be a weak broth. I can see that now. There aren't many vegetables. But I don't care. I want the warmth of it anyway, on my hands cupped around a bowl, in my belly.

They invite us to come with them. To stop our journey back to Königsberg and try again on another ship. Königsberg will soon be under siege once more by the Soviets, they say. They have just come from there. So much has been destroyed in the bombing. Already the Wehrmacht is constructing barricades to prepare for the Red Army attack that is sure to begin soon, any day now.

But we've come too far. That's what we tell ourselves—Gerhard and me. Pieta stays quiet. Even her whisper voice has gone away again. The old couple does their best to convince us, but we tell them we've made up our minds.

In the morning, they share what food they have. I know we should turn down their offer. They will need all their food to stay alive. But I can't say no. None of us can. We thank them and say goodbye.

A day later, two weeks into the crossing, Pieta develops a fever. We are in another snowstorm, but she is sweating. The sweat freezes and cracks when she moves her face and I can tell it hurts, but she doesn't complain. She falls asleep in my arms, and I hold her as the horse strains to pull us forward over the ice road. Pieta slumps against me until I shake her to make sure she's still okay. She nods, but then falls asleep again.

I bundle her up as much as I can and let her lie down with her head in my lap while Gerhard and I study the ice ahead, looking for cracks so we can give them a wide berth—and praying we're not giving up one unsafe track only to find ourselves on another.

CHAPTER 32
PIETA

I am in a ghost world. White everywhere. And gray. White and gray. The gray is the shadows. I want to lie down. I want to sleep. I want Mama to sing to me Brahms's "Lullaby." I want her to sing the lullaby for little Riki.

Mama is with me. I only can't see her, but I know she is here, nearby. And so are Opa and Oma. I wish Papa was, too, but no. He is too far away. He is not here anymore.

Asta is here. I even can hear her. If I opened my eyes again, I would see her. If I spoke again, she would hear me. I would say to her, "Asta, I am sorry. For making you hold back from your friends in Königsberg to wait for me, to keep me company. Sorry for refusing to leave the shelter after the bombing. But wasn't it good in the end that I refused to leave the shelter—because there was more bombing? Sorry for the little boy who Mama picked up and carried. I wanted her to carry me instead, and wasn't that so selfish of me? Sorry that I made you worry about me. Sorry that you had to look after me on Opa and Oma's farm."

I wish Asta wasn't so angry now. I wish she would stop shaking me. I wish she wouldn't shout at me. I wish she wouldn't slap me and make my face burn and my eyes pour out tears that freeze. I wish she would stop saying my name over and over and over. I wish she would let me sleep.

CHAPTER 33
ASTA

It is Gerhard who notices it first. "Her face! Look at her face!" No one has spoken since early morning when we began. I've been holding Pieta for hours. She is so weak. I am afraid she might fall out of the wagon. It takes me a minute to do as Gerhard says, a minute more to understand what I'm seeing—that Pieta's cheeks and nose, everything not covered by her balaclava, have turned yellow. "Slap her!" Gerhard shouts. "You must slap her. And hard." So I do. Without knowing why. But he is so certain.

Pieta opens her eyes, her teary eyes. She mumbles. She tries to lift her arms to stop me from slapping her. "Now rub!" Gerhard says. He is tying off the reins, though the horse keeps plodding forward on the track of ice and snow across the empty desert of the frozen lagoon. He seizes Pieta and pushes my hands away. He does it himself, massaging her exposed flesh while she struggles to get away from us but is too confused. She makes animal noises and calls out for Mama. The yellow slowly fades. The pink color returns to her face. He picks up the reins again. He tells me to continue massaging to keep the blood flowing back to her skin. It must be painful to Pieta because now she's crying and fighting harder to make me stop.

"It is frostbite," Gerhard says. "We have to do this. It will turn into gangrene if we don't. We have to keep her covered. All of her covered." And so I do. Panicked, I pull her into the back of the wagon, on top of the canvas and as many blankets as I can use for a bed, with all the rest on top of us. I pull them over our heads, blanking out the frozen world. I keep rubbing. I breathe my warm breath on Pieta's face. I peel off her mittens and rub her cold hands until they are warm again, too. I stay there with her, sharing the heat of my body, while Gerhard—brave, smart Gerhard, who has saved her—stays alone on the wagon bench and coaxes the tired horse on and on through the long, wintry day until night.

We stop with several other families who we meet going the other way. They have taken apart another broken wagon and set it on fire and like the old couple they let us share what they have—their stew and bread, the roaring bonfire for as long as it lasts, their company. Like so many others before, they urge us to turn around and go with them back across the Vistula Lagoon to Gotenhafen. But now we have even more urgent reason to continue to Königsberg—to find a hospital for Pieta. We have saved her from the frostbite, but she still has a fever. She drinks and drinks the water I give her from melted snow, but she can eat only a little of the food I offer. The bread sits in her mouth, unchewed, until I take it out and soften it for her and place it on her tongue again.

She mutters something that night under the layers of horse blankets that keep us from freezing but still aren't enough, aren't ever enough, to make us warm. I press my ear close to her lips and recognize the song, Brahms's "Lullaby." I think of Mama. I think of us back when we were little. Pieta is still nine and I am still eleven, but we aren't children anymore.

Gerhard, who is ten, is no longer a child, either. Even though, as happens every night when he joins us under the blankets, I still hear him cry himself to sleep.

. . . .

We are broken down. The horse can't go on. We sit. Pieta is too weak to continue on foot, though we are within sight of the shore. Distant sight. So distant I wonder if it might be a mirage, like we read about in school, in the desert, where desperate travelers were certain they saw palm trees and an oasis far off, riding through the hot, shimmering sands. Only when they got there—nothing.

But Gerhard swears he sees it, too. He will go for help, he says. For suddenly, the past day, we've encountered no other travelers, no refugee caravans. Pieta cries out in her feverish sleep. I tell Gerhard to go. So he does.

And hours later, he brings help—a German patrol. A miracle. They come in an open car of all things, driven out over the frozen lagoon. Teenagers in army uniforms. Boys we might have once seen riding bicycles through the streets of Königsberg or playing football in one of the parks. There are no Heil Hitlers here. Everyone is done with that. They have more blankets. They lift Pieta gently and place her on the back seat. Her eyes stay closed the whole time. Gerhard and I hang on to the running board. But the soldiers aren't ready to leave. They tie a rope around the horse and the other end to the back of the vehicle, then drag the carcass behind them when they drive off—slowly, even carefully, so they won't ruin the meat. We pass another line of refugees. They have just left Königsberg, the soldiers tell us. All overland travel to Germany has been severed. The trains. The roads. Everything. The frozen Vistula Lagoon is the only route left to Gotenhafen and the ships. The refugees, heads down—even the children, even the horses—hardly take notice as we pass.

Once we're off the ice, the soldiers bury the remains of the horse under a thin blanket of snow and mark the spot with a small flag. They will return with a butcher from town and a truck, they tell us. Everything is in short supply. Nothing can be wasted.

The driver, who looks so young I wonder if he can even be a teenager, adjusts the blankets over Pieta. It is a kind gesture. I have almost forgotten already about kindness.

"Now to the hospital," he says. And we go.

CHAPTER 34
PIETA

The hospital is warm. Even with the shattered windows. Even with the snow drift at one end of the ward where the boards have fallen in. Gerhard the Barnacle says if he can only find a hammer and nails, he will refasten them. But if all the windows are boarded up, there will be no light. The electricity comes and goes. Bombs still rain down on the city. That's what the nurses say. I hear them in passing. They don't have time to spend with their patients. They give medicine until they run out. They tend to wounds. They change dressings. They pile on more blankets when I can't stop shivering, when I swing from sweating with fever to freezing with fever and I don't know why. They stuff rags and cardboard in the broken windows. They give me medicine that makes me sleep. But it doesn't make the fever go away. Sometimes I can't stop shaking. If Asta is here, she climbs in the bed with me. At night she sleeps with me. The

Barnacle sleeps on the floor. I share my blankets. There is little to eat. In the morning, there is bread sprinkled with a pinch of sugar. If there is no bread, then sometimes a piece of hard candy. Asta tells me not to bite it. She says to let it dissolve in my mouth so it will last longer. At noon and evening are cups of broth. Some of the children peel paper off the walls to eat. Pieta and Gerhard the Barnacle go out in the streets to beg for food. They bring it back to share with me, but I never see them eat. Asta finds potato peels in a garbage pit somewhere in the city. She sticks them to the sides of the potbelly stove and when they fall off, she collects them from the floor and announces that they're ready and gives them to me. I make her promise me that she is also eating, even if I don't see her. The Barnacle, too. They have to work so hard for everything. Asta says in all of Königsberg, there are no stores selling food anymore. There are no restaurants. There are no sidewalk carts. There are only hungry people. Hungry soldiers. Hungry children.

The nurses are always tired. They sleep on cots in a corner of the ward but never for very long. Someone always needs them. Someone is crying. Someone can't breathe. Someone is calling for her mother and it's the middle of the night and they're so loud that others yell at them to stop. Someone yells something cruel: "Your mother is dead."

One night Mama comes onto the ward. I see her at the far end, the snowdrift end. She is standing in a yellow light. She doesn't speak. She only stands. But she has no face. That's what upsets me. How will I ever remember her face if I can't see it anymore, even now that she has come to the hospital to see me? She walks toward me and I'm so happy that I will get to be with her again. She walks and walks, but she never gets any closer. The ward stretches away from my bed. The yellow light grows brighter around her, then dimmer. I start to see her face, the outline of her face, but the light by now has gotten so dim that it's no use and then the light is gone and so is Mama.

I hear Asta, next to me in the dark, saying, "It's all right, Pieta. It's all right. Don't cry. Don't cry."

I tell her Mama was here. I saw her, but I didn't see her face. Asta might be crying, too. She says again, "It's all right Pieta. Don't cry."

Three more children die in the night. Bombs explode all over the city. The remaining windows on the ward that weren't broken before are shattered now, glass everywhere, on the floor, on the beds. Snow blows in from the howling wind outside. There is no one to bring in more boards. No one with a hammer and nails. Soldiers bring stretchers onto the ward with people who are bleeding and some who have stopped bleeding and stopped breathing. They leave them on the floor. Only later, hours later, does a doctor come, and more nurses, to bandage them, or to cover their faces with blankets. An old priest, who mumbles to himself, also comes onto the ward. He stops at my bed and says he has come to pray for us. I ask him if he will pray for Mama.

He looks around. "And where is your mother?"

"Gone," I whisper.

The fever has given me my whisper voice back, even with a stranger.

The old priest nods. "Of course I will pray for her," he says. "And I will pray for you, too."

"And Asta," I add. "And Gerhard. And Opa and Oma. And the Müllers. And Fedde."

I stop, afraid I've asked for too much—too many prayers for too many people. And one horse.

"All of them," he assures me. "All the living and all the dead, too."

CHAPTER 35
ASTA

"We can't stay any longer, Pieta," I tell her. She's awake, and I think she understands what I'm saying. Some days she does, some days she doesn't. She's told me she saw Mama on the ward and a yellow light, about a priest who came to see her and promised he would say a prayer for Fedde, and that they brought soldiers and other bombing victims in on stretchers and left them here. That one might have been true. There is blood on the floor that no one has cleaned. A lot of blood. And discarded bandages. And remnants of uniforms. But if there were stretchers, they've been taken away. It's impossible to know what Pieta sees and what she imagines seeing when we're not here.

"On the streets they're saying the Red Army has surrounded the city," I say. "Nearly all the civilians have fled. There is no one left to give us food except the soldiers, and they are starving, too."

Most of the doctors and nurses and other workers have left the hospital, but I don't tell Pieta that. I don't know why. She should have already noticed. But maybe with the fevers, she hasn't. The children on the ward have been separated from their parents, lost in the evacuation. Some are no longer breathing, but there's no one to cover their faces, and no blankets to cover them with, anyway. People steal the blankets. But probably it's not stealing if no one is using them. The dead don't need blankets.

I tell Pieta that Gerhard is still out begging on the streets. Yesterday he stole some bread from an open Wehrmacht truck and a soldier chased him and caught him. Gerhard got away when the soldiers seized the bread and yanked it out of his hands. Gerhard was left with only a crust, but he still shared it with me, and I shared mine with Pieta. Later, Gerhard found a small bag of Ersatzkaffee, the powdered coffee substitute that Mama and everyone drank, which he found some way to brew, and then drink. And then, because there wasn't anything else, we ate the grounds.

I don't tell Pieta this. And I don't tell her that we found the military records office. It, too, has been destroyed in the bombing, and now there's no way we'll ever be able to find Papa.

"We will go to Gerhard's farm," I say to Pieta. "Maybe his aunt and uncle will still be there. But even if his aunt and uncle are gone, we can stay there. We can build a fire. There is plenty of wood in the forest. Gerhard can trap rabbits and hares. He knows how to do that.

We can dig up the buried potatoes. In the spring, we can plant more things. And when the Red Army goes away, we can come to Königsberg again and find Papa when he is back from the war."

Pieta struggles to sit up. Her face is bathed in sweat. I am worried about what will happen to her when we travel. I don't think she can walk. I don't know if Gerhard will be able to find a cart for us to carry her. I don't know how we will get out of Königsberg now that the Wehrmacht soldiers have turned it into a fortress with makeshift walls and rolls of wire and guns and cannons. I don't know how Pieta will be able to weave her way with us through streets that are almost impassable with so many bomb craters and broken bricks and shattered glass and fallen buildings and towers. And bodies of people and animals. But I worry even more that if she stays here on the hospital ward with no food and no medicine and no one left to take care of her except me and Gerhard that she will die.

I tell Pieta it will only take a few days to get to the farm, and I tell her again and again, as if I'm trying to convince myself, that we will be safe and warm when we get there. And please, please, please, please, God, let Gerhard find a cart so we can pull Pieta and she can ride and we can keep her safe and warm on the journey.

CHAPTER 36
PIETA

Gerhard the Barnacle is waiting on the street outside the hospital. I am leaning on Asta's arm, both of us gripping as many blankets as we can carry with our free hands. But even that makes me tired. I have become so weak. I say this to Asta, and apologize. She takes my blankets and adds them to her own bundle.

"It's all right, Pieta," she says. "You won't have to walk. Look." She points next to the Barnacle. He has found a hand cart so I can sit and ride. "We will take turns pulling," she says, when I protest. "It won't be hard. We need it to carry everything else, too."

The Barnacle smiles, but it's a tired smile. "I am sorry there is no whip so you can make us go faster," he says. It's meant to be a joke, but I think I have forgotten how to laugh, even to be polite.

I insist that I can walk, and I try, but I slip in the snow as soon as we are only one block away from the hospital. They help me climb into the cart and we continue. I know I should be shocked and horrified by what I see—the remains of the city, even worse than after the first bombing. Lifeless people in the streets. No one to bury them. Instead, I am numb. Instead, in the cart, under the blankets, I try not to look. Asta and Gerhard are so brave. They march on. They keep their eyes open. Even before we leave the city, more planes fly overhead and more bombs are dropped and Asta and Gerhard carry me to a shelter. We follow the crowd running there. That's how we know where to go. None of the landmarks of the Königsberg that we used to know are still standing. Most of the bridges are gone. We keep having to turn around when the street stops at the river's edge and we can go no farther. Maybe we should try crossing over the ice when the bombing stops. Like the ice we crossed all those many, many freezing days on the Vistula Lagoon, frozen as hard as the earth.

But before we can find a way across the river and out of the city, the bombing starts again. Asta and Gerhard lift me from the cart as if I'm a bundle of rags and carry me to a nearby shelter. Suddenly there are people all around us, pouring down the stairs into a reinforced basement like the one that saved Asta and Mama and me so long ago. We force our way inside and press against a back wall. I try to stand, but my legs give out and I sag to the damp floor. Asta and Gerhard sit with me and hold me up.

The bunker shakes. Dust and debris rain down on us from the

ceiling. A woman sitting nearby begins talking loudly, over the sounds of the bombs exploding. At first I can't make out what she's saying. I can tell she's upset. Everyone is afraid, but she is the most afraid. A man sits next to her, leaning against the wall, his eyes closed. Perhaps he is her husband. He doesn't say anything as she shouts at him, as if no one else is hiding down here in the shelter. As if no one else can hear.

"How long can we stay here?" she says to him. "You promised it was safest if we stayed, but look at us now! The whole city is in ruins. Everyone has already left. Everyone who had sense to see what is happening. And where can we go now? The Red Army is five kilometers away. Five kilometers! They are bombing the Vistula route. They are bombing the ports in Pillau. In Gotenhafen. They are sinking the ships of the evacuation. The Wehrmacht defenders—they are schoolboys! We are doomed here."

Someone says "Please, Fräulein. There are children here."

But she keeps shouting. "The children need to know! The Soviets show no mercy to anyone. You have all heard the stories! Not even children are spared. Not even the old. We have all heard what they are doing to the women. They are monsters!"

"Fräulein!" the voice says from another corner of the shelter. "Enough!"

And she stops. We sit in silence, listening to the bombing that is now in the distance, growing fainter. The ground is no longer shaking. Plaster no longer rains down on our heads, shaken loose from the ceiling. Asta has been squeezing my hand the whole time. Or perhaps I have been squeezing hers. But I am so weak. It hurts either way. But I don't want to let go. I don't want her to let go. Gerhard is muttering to himself. Asta asks him what he is saying, but he only shakes his head, so she leaves him alone. He is the opposite of the woman in the shelter, the woman who was shouting so everyone had to listen. The woman whose husband, we realize only after the air raid sirens cease and the bombing ends altogether and the shelter door is dragged open and the gray winter light is let in, has stopped breathing.

· · · · · · · · · · ·

When we reach the barricade around the city, the young guards at first refuse to let us pass. Asta pleads with them, then she argues with them, then she raises her voice and shouts at them. They blink, listening to her, this young girl who has gotten so angry so quickly. One shrugs and lets us through.

Gerhard is pulling the cart, first on an empty highway, dodging potholes and burned cars and wagons. Then, after a few hours, we turn onto a narrower road. I fall asleep. I wake. Asta checks on me, gives me water to drink. I insist that she have some, too, her and Gerhard. I decide I cannot call him the Barnacle anymore. From now on I will think of him as only Gerhard. I am ashamed that I was unkind in how I thought of him before. Ashamed that I told Asta he was Gerhard the Barnacle. I know now that I was jealous of him. Asta makes friends so easily. She made friends with Monika. She made friends with Gerhard. I only hope that we don't lose him, too.

CHAPTER 37
ASTA

We're two days getting to the farmhouse. Two days taking turns pulling the cart with Pieta. Halfway through the second day, as Gerhard and I are pushing and pulling the cart, trying to free it from a frozen rut in a road that seems to be nothing but ruts, deep tracks left by military trucks and wagons and tanks, Pieta climbs out and walks. Just like that. Gerhard and I stop what we're doing and look at her. She takes a few tentative steps, and then stops, turns, looks back at us. She starts to return, maybe to help, but I tell her to keep going and wait for us ahead until we work the cart loose and can join her. She has a blanket wrapped around her and it drags in the mud and snow, but I'm so happy to see that she has the strength to walk that I don't say anything. And I probably wouldn't say anything, anyway. Mama used to tease me for insisting that everything must be so neat and tidy. I hated for anything to be out of its place—my schoolbooks, my dolls, my things. But somewhere along the way, since leaving Königsberg the first time, all those months ago, I've lost that part of myself. Now I'm almost the opposite. I chop my hair short, and Pieta's hair, too, so that if we run into Red Army soldiers they'll think we're all boys, dirty, poor, not worth their time to hurt or kill.

But so far we've only seen other refugees, most of them going north to the port of Pillau, where the woman in the shelter said the Allies were bombing, but the Red Army hasn't yet reached, so there are still some refugee ships risking the Baltic passage.

"Are you sure you can walk?" I ask Pieta once we've wrestled the cart free. It's so much lighter now without her in it, not that Pieta, or any of the three of us, weigh very much anymore. We're all so thin. Not like skeletons—at least not with our oversized clothes and heavy coats—but nearly so.

Pieta nods. Sometimes she uses her whisper voice since she got it back. Sometimes she doesn't. I tell her she should ride anyway, that it's not much farther now. I look to Gerhard for confirmation. At first he nods. But then he shakes his head.

Pieta draws the blanket tighter around her and refuses to get back in the cart, and so we continue, moving as slowly with a weak Pieta walking under her own power as we were when she was in the cart.

The snow continues, so hard at times that we're forced to stop and crouch beneath the cart until it eases and the wind dies back down, and we can press on again. I think it is still February, but I can't be certain. I lost track of the days during the Vistula crossing and never bothered to ask when we reached Königsberg. We were too busy finding help for Pieta and finding food.

Gerhard is bolder in that way. He will pick through garbage. He will ask anyone for help. He will hold out his hand in a way that he expects it will be filled, even with an apple peel, a crust of bread, a single coin, not that there is anything left to buy even if we had a hundred coins. I am embarrassed, though I follow his lead and force myself to beg, because what else is there to do to stay alive? We saw what the children were doing in the hospital, the ones who could get out of their beds: taking not only the strips of wallpaper to chew and swallow, but also paper, straw, handfuls of snow. Anything to stop their bellies from rumbling and complaining.

Anything to stop our own.

· · · · · · · · · ·

When we finally reach the farmhouse, we are happy to see that it is still standing. Inside it is cold, is freezing, but Gerhard and I quickly set to work bringing in wood and filling the fireplace and the black potbelly stove. Pieta is so exhausted that she falls asleep in the living room on a bear rug we drag over for her in front of the fire. We cover her with blankets. I find pots in the kitchen and a pump that still works just outside the door, the handle miraculously not frozen. Soon we have hot water and a few potatoes Gerhard has found in the bottom of a storage bin. There is little else in the house. Most of the furniture has been taken or destroyed. The pantry is empty but for a few jars of pickled beets. Some carrots. I cut them all up and boil everything together.

We eat in front of the fireplace, the three of us, finally warm. The house is silent but for the wind blowing outside. The fire is smoky and the smoke soon hovers over us on the ceiling like a cloud, but we don't care. It's dark out, fully night, and we're safe. That's all I know. Tomorrow Gerhard and I will explore the property. He has been here dozens of times before, but never alone, and never when it was abandoned. He doesn't know what has become of his aunt and uncle. Maybe they are hiding in the nearby Memel Forest. Maybe they changed their minds after the rest of his family left. Maybe they, too, joined the evacuation.

He doesn't want to talk about what else might have happened to them, just as I don't want to think about Papa and where he might be, and if he's still alive, and how he will ever find us if he manages to survive the war.

CHAPTER 38
PIETA

We sleep together on the rug by the fire, the wonderful, wonderful fire. Asta was so proud of me today, and I was proud of me also. Gerhard—who can say? He speaks to Asta. He listens to her. He stays busy. Always busy. During the night I wake up and see him. He rolls out of the blankets and goes to the window and stares for the longest time out over the white, rolling fields. The moon is full. I can see it in how bright everything is, reflecting off the snow. I get up, too, careful not to wake Asta. I pull on my coat. We all sleep in our boots and our clothes as we've done for the past months since the hunt. The fire has died down, but the embers still glow red and orange.

I stand next to Gerhard, but I don't say anything. I think he might be lonely, but at the same time he might not want to be disturbed because he will feel as though he has to make conversation.

I'm the same way most of the time. He is muttering to himself until he hears me come up. He looks down at me and says, "Hi, Pieta." Then he turns his face back toward the window and the view of the fields and the snow and the moon and the far away, dark tree line. It is beautiful. I remember Mama saying that sometimes if you are quiet and if you are still and if you let yourself just look and see, then whatever is in front of you, even if you've seen it a million times, can seem wonderful and new. I wonder if that's how this is for Gerhard. It makes me happy just to be standing here with him—this boy who has lost everything but has still worked so hard to help us—and seeing this picture of a field covered with fresh snow under a full moon as if neither of us has ever seen such a thing before.

Only that's not what he's looking at, after all. "Do you see?" he asks.

I force my whisper voice to answer. "The field?"

"No," he says. "Beyond the field. In the trees. Do you see something moving?"

I stare harder where he says. I stare and stare until my eyes water. Until I realize I am cold standing here and suddenly afraid. But I don't see anything moving. I don't see anything at all. I just see shadows and light, and the shadows are a mystery. I rub my eyes and return to staring, and now *everything* seems to be moving, shimmering, trembling. Only I'm the one who is trembling. I pull my coat tighter around me. Gerhard is trembling, too. He doesn't have his coat on. How cold must he be?

I tug on his sleeve and point to the fire. He has made a woodpile inside the door against the wall. He tells me to hold out my arms and he loads them up with wood. He loads his own arms. I follow him back to the fireplace and soon the fire is leaping again.

"Do you know about the Forest Brothers?" Gerhard asks me when we are settled on our blankets, close to the warm flames. I shake my head.

"Are they monsters?" I ask. "Was that what we saw at the tree line?"

"Not monsters," he says. "Except to the communists."

I know about the communists. In the Soviet Union they are all communists. We learned about them in school.

"The Forest Brothers are Lithuanian freedom fighters who live here, in the forest, on either side of the Memel River. They want to drive away the communists. They also want to drive away the Germans. They hate Stalin in the Soviet Union and they also hate Hitler in Germany."

"But why?" I ask.

"They want the Lithuanian people to be left alone." Gerhard shrugs. "That's why the Forest Brothers hide here. So they can come out to fight when they want, and so they can hide when they want. My uncle and my aunt sometimes gave them food.

Sometimes let them sleep in the barn. One time they even took care of one of the Forest Brothers who had been shot. But he died, anyway."

"Will they come here?" I ask.

"I don't know," Gerhard says. "But they've been watching us."

CHAPTER 39
ASTA

The following week keeps us busy. At first, we despair that everything is gone—taken, sold, stolen, destroyed, who can say? All the livestock in the barn: gone. All the food in the pantry: gone. The beds, the tables, the chairs, most of the furniture: gone, some of it burned in a pile outside between the farmhouse and the barn. Gerhard looks at it for a long time. He looks at many things on the farm for a long time. I ask him what he's thinking, but he only shakes his head. I tell myself he must be remembering all the times he was here with his aunt and uncle and his family, and everything gone is a reminder to him, a painful reminder, of their absence. He tells me about the Forest Brothers he thinks he saw in the middle of the night. Gerhard says they won't hurt us, but I don't know how he can be so sure, even if his aunt and uncle were kind to them at times.

To me they are just one more thing I have to worry about.

In the field we dig up a few potatoes and beets, sorry remnants that escaped the harvest but that we'll keep and eat because there is little else. Pieta tries to follow us, but I insist that she stay inside. Her fever has broken, and she's already so much better, but I don't want her to get sick again. At the hospital, a doctor told us Pieta was suffering from pleurisy, an inflammation in her chest and lungs, and perhaps pneumonia.

"You need to keep the fire burning," I tell her. "Don't use all the wood. Just enough so the room is warm." We have hung horse blankets from the barn to block off the other rooms and keep the heat in the living room and kitchen. The blankets, and some old clothes upstairs, are among the few things left by Gerhard's aunt and uncle.

"But I want to help, too," Pieta whispers. I'm still surprised that she is speaking again. I even heard her say something quietly to Gerhard, and he spoke to her, too. She doesn't call him the Barnacle and I'm glad about that, but to be honest, I also miss her calling him that. I tried not to laugh when she said it, but sometimes I couldn't help myself. Of course, it wasn't nice of either of us, but as long as it was a sister secret, and as long as he didn't hear it and have his feelings hurt, maybe that made it okay.

"This is the best way to help," I tell Pieta. "And not getting sick again. Gerhard and I have to go into the woods to set snares for rabbits. He knows how to do this, and he's going to teach me and I'm going to help him."

Pieta's eyes widen. "Rabbits?"

I look at her with my sternest face. "We have to eat, Pieta. You have to eat. And you have to eat what we can find. You will get sick again if you don't. So promise me."

She looks doubtful, so I say it again.

"Promise me. Promise me you won't make a fuss. Promise me that you will eat whatever we can catch."

I don't know why I feel I have to convince Pieta to eat. We're all hungry. Her stomach is rumbling as loudly as mind and Gerhard's. The boiled vegetables from last night made for a weak soup that hardly filled us. We have been famished for days. For weeks. *Of course* Pieta will eat whatever we catch.

She nods, and off I go with Gerhard.

. . . .

It doesn't take him long to find a rabbit trail. He points down at the paw prints in the snow. There are several sets, dusted over by a recent snowfall, but still visible, winding through trees and winter brush in dark woods on the far side of the fields. We follow them for a while until the trail narrows between a large stone and a fallen tree.

"Here is the best place," Gerhard says, and he sets to work. He has brought thin wire he found in the barn that he twists into a loop the size of his fist. He has me cut down a sapling, which he lays like a bridge from the trunk of the fallen tree to a crack in the stone, wedging the sapling in as tightly as he can so it won't be knocked out or pulled loose. He winds the wire several times around the narrow trunk so the loop can hang down over the trail, almost invisible, at the height of a rabbit's head.

"Done," he says, and he stands back to admire his work.

"That's it?" I ask. "Don't you need to leave some food? A carrot? Some sort of bait?"

Gerhard grins. "No. Why would we do that? Herr Rabbit, he hops along the trail. He ducks under the tree. His head goes in the snare. He can't get out. The wire is tied off here, so what can he do? The more he tries to get away, the more the wire tightens so he can't. And then he becomes our dinner."

I tell him that's what I thought, as if I've done this many times before, but I just forgot. I don't want him to think I'm squeamish. But then I have another thought.

"And you will do what with the fur? And the parts we can see?" I mean the rabbit's head. His ears and eyes and all the rest.

Gerhard shows me his knife.

• • • • • • • • • •

It's three days before a rabbit sticks his head in the wire loop and can't get it out. Three days of tramping through the woods with Gerhard to check and coming back empty—to Pieta's relief. Three days of eating potatoes and the last of the beets. The rabbit is still struggling when we find it. Gerhard smashes its head with a rock and then we take it back to the barn where he skins it and guts it. I have watched Opa's workers do this, but never up close. I hold a bucket. Gerhard throws in the heart, the liver, the kidneys. In another bucket, he drains the rabbit's blood. He tells me to find somewhere to hang up the pelt so it can dry. The head he tells me to save. And all the bones. I try to act as though it's no big deal, but it's all so disgusting that I can hardly bring myself to watch.

"My aunt boiled them," he explains. "To make a broth. Then you add everything."

"You mean potatoes?" I ask. Because we don't have anything else.

He shrugs. "She always grew things in her garden." He gestures outside, but if there's a garden there anymore, it's buried in snow. "Anyway, she said it is sinful to waste. So we should use everything from the rabbit."

"The blood?"

"For gravy, I think. And sausage. Blood sausage. You need to squeeze out what's inside the intestines and then you can use them to make the sausage. You fill them up with meat and blood and spices and onions and peppers and grains."

He stops. Most of that we don't have. But there, next to the barn wall, is a meat grinder. "We can use that," he says. "If there's anything left over from what we cook tonight."

But there isn't. Even Pieta eats everything we give her. We cook potato peels in lard. Pan fry the rabbit's legs. Boil the head and the ribs until the meat is gone and the water is a rich, dark brown. We find some flour and stir it in with the rabbit blood, but the proportions are all wrong and it's a thick red sludge that I start to throw out, but Gerhard stops me.

The next day we add potatoes to the broth.

The day after that it's the liver and kidney and heart we fry in the skillet.

On the third day, with nothing else left of the rabbit, and no more rabbits caught in Gerhard's snare, we eat the red sludge.

CHAPTER 40
PIETA

Thunder shakes the farmhouse. I feel it inside me. I feel it at night when I'm supposed to be asleep. Asta says don't worry, don't worry it's so far away. It's the war. It's the bombs. She says they're not coming here. Why would they come here? Why would they care about a little farmhouse on a little farm at the edge of the forest on the Memel River? Why would they care about the three of us?

Only there aren't three of us anymore. I am sure now that I see the Forest Brothers from time to time, sometimes at night, sometimes in the day, when I stand at the window and stare at the tree line. I haven't stopped since that night with Gerhard, since he asked if I saw something moving. And now I think I do. Sometimes. And Gerhard, too, says he saw tracks in the snow coming across the field to the farm. Asta asks him if they could be animal tracks and not people tracks. The snow has covered them—not all the way but enough that it's hard to tell. Even Gerhard says this.

So I keep watch. During the day when Asta and Gerhard disappear into the woods to check on their rabbit traps. When they dig and dig in the field to find more potatoes and beets that escaped the harvest and we can still eat. And at night while they sleep.

And still there is the thunder. And on clear nights the lightning, too, which Gerhard and Asta say are explosions from the bombs—there, in the west, from Königsberg, and there, to the north, in Pillau. "They're bombing the port," Gerhard says, pointing, as if I can't see if for myself like the northern lights dancing across the night sky.

One night, when none of us can sleep, Asta asks Gerhard how often he came here to the farm.

He is quiet for a long time before he finally says, "Every summer. And also every Christmas. My mother sent me. Anytime I wasn't in school. I don't think she wanted me around."

"That can't be true," Asta says.

"Why?" I ask him.

"She worked all the time, in the munitions factory during the day," he says. "And she also worked at night, at a café. There were singers and dancers there. Sometimes she didn't come home."

"But where was your father?" I ask. "Was he gone in the army?"

Gerhard says he doesn't know. "Mama wouldn't tell me. She wouldn't talk about him. She only told me he left us when I was a little boy."

"And he never came back?"

Gerhard shakes his head. "And I'm glad. Because the other men who came to see Mama, they always brought me presents. One even gave me this knife."

He holds up the blade he's been using for skinning rabbits, cutting wire, everything. The knife he used to cut the cable holding our lifeboat back on the *Wilhelm Gustloff.*

"You were lucky to have your aunt and uncle," Asta says.

Gerhard scowls. "I wish they had let me stay with them. They made me go with Mama to Gotenhafen. Mama wasn't even with me when the torpedoes hit the ship. I don't know where she was. I was alone on the deck. I don't know what happened to her."

"We don't know what happened to our mother, either," I say quietly. But that's not true. We can pretend, but we all know.

· · · · · · · · · · ·

A few nights later, the Forest Brothers come to the farm, several ragged men trudging across the field. I am standing alone at the window, watching. The snow has started up, but I can still see they carry guns and rifles slung over their shoulders. They wear ushankas, the Soviet fur hats, the flaps pulled tightly down over their ears, and long, heavy wool coats to their knees, and ammunition belts crisscrossing their chests, and packs strapped high on their backs.

I wake up Asta and Gerhard.

"We should run," Asta says.

Gerhard shakes his head. "It would be too late, anyway," he replies as the men make their way now into the frozen farmyard.

They don't bother to knock. The door opens, letting in the wind and snow—and the men. One of them speaks in a language I don't know while another closes the door. Asta hugs me. Gerhard steps in front of us, as if he is our protector. The men laugh and shrug and drop their packs on the floor. They light candles. They warm themselves at the fire. They pull out food from their packs. Dried meat. Flasks. Sacks of grain. Potatoes. One busies himself at the stove. Two of them pick up their rifles and go back outside to stand guard. I can see them at different corners of the barn, half-hidden. We stay huddled together until one of the men waves at us to sit. When their meal is ready, they hand us bowls of food. We eat quickly with our hands because there have been no rabbits for days and we have had nothing in our bellies, and in no time the bowls are empty and we lick them clean. The men laugh at us again, but it is a tired laugh. They drink from their flasks. Two men go outside to replace the guards, who come inside for their meal.

The Forest Brothers roll out their sleeping bags on the floor but let us keep our bed on the bear rug next to the fire. Their snoring is so loud that I think I will never fall asleep, even when I have decided they are not going to hurt us, but finally I do, and in the morning, like magic, they are gone.

CHAPTER 41
ASTA

We are in luck! Our snares catch not one but two rabbits. We have had nothing to eat for three days since the Forest Brothers came, and now we will have a feast! Gerhard and I show Pieta through the kitchen window and for once she doesn't make a face. She is as hungry as we are.

"Today is your turn," Gerhard says when we make our way to the barn. He hands me his knife. "You've seen how I do it. Now you."

I don't even hesitate. The time for being squeamish is long past. I make a cut in the fur halfway down the rabbit's back, work my fingers inside, and pull half the fur all the way off in one direction, over the hind legs and tail, and the other half of the fur all the way off in the other direction, over the front legs and head. Like taking off the rabbit's pants and coat. And then there's all the rest, which takes a lot longer than you'd think for such a small animal, one that looks even smaller once it's stripped down to the meat.

I'm just finishing with the first rabbit when Gerhard looks over at the partially open barn door.

"What is it?" I ask. "Did you hear something?"

He nods and goes to the door for a better look, out across the fields. He squints into the morning sun. It's cold out—there's fresh snow from last night—but the clouds have passed for the moment. "They're back," he says. "The Forest Brothers." And he goes out to greet them.

I wipe my hands on a rag and follow him, but before I reach the door, I hear a popping sound. And then several more popping sounds. I step outside but don't see Gerhard anywhere. A dozen men in uniforms are coming toward us, their guns raised, still half a field away but close enough for me to see the red Soviet stars on their caps.

I run to the farmhouse for Pieta, grab her arm and some blankets, race back out the door with her and away. More popping sounds follow us. We run and run and run. I am dragging Pieta. She protests. I force her to keep running through more fields behind the farmhouse, away from the soldiers. I look back, expecting to see them closing in, but they haven't followed us. Maybe they stopped at the farmhouse. Maybe they're chasing Gerhard. I feel a surge of panic at the thought. We plunge into the forest and keep running through snow drifts and around trees until our breathing is too ragged to continue and I think we've made ourselves invisible.

I wrap the two blankets around Pieta and me. I'm still holding Gerhard's bloody knife.

I think Pieta will start crying, but she doesn't. She shouts at me: "Where is Gerhard? Why did we leave him?"

"There wasn't time," I say, straining to see if the Red Army soldiers are following us. "I didn't see him when I came out of the barn. The soldiers were already shooting. We had to run."

"But we left him," Pieta says again, this time with sadness in her voice.

"I'm sorry," I say. "We'll go back once it's safe. We'll find him. I know we will." Once again I have to pretend everything will be okay. But inside, I'm so scared for Gerhard, and so worried that he's been hurt, that it's all I can do to keep from crying myself.

Pieta hugs me for a long time and won't let go as we sit at the base of a sheltering birch tree. I make a tent over us with the blankets and dig a snow cave like Mama taught us and pray that the Red Army soldiers don't find us here. Pieta says a prayer out loud for Gerhard. "Please let him be safe and hiding like us. Please don't let him be hurt."

I pray for him, too, silently, in my heart.

"It's good I didn't see him," I tell Pieta. "When I followed him out of the barn. That means he got away."

Pieta nods. I feel her head move against my shoulder. We both want to believe it so much that we decide it must be true.

After awhile, after my heart stops racing, after my breath no longer comes in sharp gasps from all the running and the adrenaline and the fear, I think about the rabbits. Not Gerhard anymore, but the rabbits. The one I skinned and cleaned so it was ready for the pan and soon would have been ready for us to eat. And the other one, saved for later. I think about the broths that would have warmed us and filled out bellies. The bones cracked open for the marrow. The organs. We wouldn't have been hungry again, or not too hungry, for days.

But now . . . now we have nothing. No wire for more snares. No dry clothes. No shelter. No Gerhard. Just these two blankets. Just this knife. Just the cover of the Memel Forest. Just each other.

CHAPTER 42
PIETA

For two days we are freezing in the forest, hiding under logs, in snow caves, one night in a real cave, the driest place of all, but I can't sleep there and neither can Asta. There could be bears hibernating deeper in the cave, and what if they wake up and find us? There could be bears out foraging in the snow for berries that they won't find because it's winter, and when they come back they'll also find us, and then what will they eat?

If Gerhard was here, he would know what to do. He would know about the bears. He would know where best for us to hide. Only now—what if there's no Gerhard anymore? How can we survive without him to help us? And what if he's hurt and he's the one who needs *us*? I can't bear to think about him out there, alone, injured. Even dead. I press my gloves to my temples and try and try to squeeze out the bad thoughts.

For two days we eat snow and sometimes bark off the pine trees. Asta says I should hold it in my mouth and let the sticky sap soften and melt before I try to swallow. She says to chew and chew the bark itself until it, too, is softened. But it never softens. It cuts my tongue. It dries out my mouth no matter how much snow I stuff in with it. I can't feel my hands and my feet and neither can Asta. She says we have to do something because we will soon have frostbite and slapping each other the way she and Gerhard did to me that time won't fix anything.

That is why she says we should go back to the farmhouse—to see if the soldiers are gone. To see if Gerhard has returned. To wait for him if not. To see if we can go back inside and build another fire and start over again.

"Come on, Pieta," Asta says, tugging at my arm. "Come *on*. We have to keep moving. We have to keep warm."

I don't like her pulling on me, and I jerk my arm away and stop walking. I cross my arms. Asta stops, too, and turns to look at me. She starts to say something but then doesn't. I know I'm being a baby and pouting and being stubborn for no good reason, but I'm sick of her bossing me around. I'm sick of being so cold and running and hiding. I'm mostly the sickest of being hungry and my stomach always rumbling, even waking me up sometimes. I'm sick of snow and bark and nowhere to get warm.

I think Asta is going to try to be sweet the way she usually does.

Maybe she has a crust of bread she's been keeping from me that she'll pull out now to get me to keep walking. Maybe she saved one of the hard candies they gave us at the hospital when there wasn't anything else for breakfast. Maybe—

But no. She just says, "Fine. Stay there." And she spins back around and stomps off through the snow.

I wait until she's out of sight, until I'm afraid she's not coming back for me, and then I follow her, now madder than before because I can't believe she has left me. I even say her name. I even shout her name, and my voice frightens me the way it echoes in the still woods. I wait, but she doesn't say anything back. I shout her name again—"ASTA!"—but still nothing. I wade faster through the snow, following her footprints, now worried, and I'm just about to shout again, a third time, when she jumps out from behind a tree and tackles me and we tumble together into the snow like kittens or puppies playing instead of sisters fighting.

"Got you!" Asta exclaims. "Gefunden!" Now sitting on top of me, as if it's been a game all along, two silly girls playing Verstecken instead of hide-and-seek in the frozen forest from Red Army soldiers and their guns.

· · · · · · · · · · ·

We creep up to the edge of the forest, across the empty fields from the farmhouse and the barn. We have smelled the smoke for a long time and now we see the farmhouse has been burned down. Only the brick walls and brick chimney are left standing. Asta says, "Why did they burn it? There's no one there anymore."

But there is someone. Even in the fading light of this late afternoon I can see Gerhard, sitting next to the barn that has been partly burned down, too.

Asta runs across the field to him, and I follow as fast as I can. We are both shouting his name, and when he hears us, he struggles to his feet and waves.

There are rags wound around his hands. His clothes are burned. His eyebrows and his hair singed. But he is smiling and shouting our names now, too. We hug him in our joy and relief and he cries out in pain.

We quickly let him go and take a step back to see what's wrong and only then do we see the damage done by the fire.

CHAPTER 43
ASTA

Gerhard is the first to speak. "I thought I had lost you!" he says. "I didn't know where you were. And everything happened so fast. I tried to look for you, but these burns . . ."

He trails off. Shows us his hands. I unwrap the rags to see. Much of the flesh is gone. Some scabs have formed, but not enough to seal off the blood and pus. Pieta looks away while I carefully wrap Gerhard's hands again. Even that light touch makes him squirm in pain. In the past, I would have looked away, too. But now—now it's different. As awful as the burns look, I know I have to do something to help Gerhard. We need him to get better. I can't let myself think about anything else.

"I'm sorry," I tell him. He tells us he's sorry, too, for leaving us behind. "As soon as I saw they were Red Army it was too late to hide," he says. "I just ran. I was so scared. But I should have stayed with you. I should have warned you."

His eyes fill with tears. Pieta is the one who tells him not to cry.

She drapes one of her blankets over his shoulders. We have moved inside the remains of the barn and are sitting on a wood pallet. The barn reeks of smoke and burnt wood, but at least it's dry and out of the wind and snow.

"We must have gone the opposite way from you," Pieta says. "Asta came and got me. We were hiding in the forest. We dug a snow cave, like our mother showed us. And we ate bark."

She makes a gagging sound, but it's just pretend.

"I have been in my own cave," Gerhard says. He lifts his head and nods above us toward the hayloft. "Under all the straw up there. But it wasn't very warm. I've been shivering the whole time, except when I was trying to put out the fire."

I ask him if that's how he burned his hands and his eyebrows and hair and the holes in his coat. But of course it is. "The soldiers didn't even bother to chase me," he says. "Once I realized, I hid over there and watched them from the trees." He indicates the direction again by nodding his head. There are woods on all sides of the farm past the fields.

"Why did they burn down the farmhouse?" Pieta asks.

Gerhard shrugs. "They just did. They filled their canteens with water from the pump. Then they threw a torch inside the barn and left. The house was already on fire and there was nothing I could do. But the barn fire was just starting. I got a blanket and tried to beat out the flames. I found a shovel and threw snow on the fire. When a section of the barn fell in, I dragged the posts away. That was how I burned my hands."

"You saved the barn!" Pieta says.

Gerhard shrugs. "Some of it, anyway."

"Enough for us to still have a place to stay," I say. Pieta tells Gerhard he is a hero and he blushes, embarrassed, but I can tell he likes her saying that.

• • • • • • • • • •

For the next few days, we eat rabbit. It's not much—the remnants of the ones we caught the morning the Red Army soldiers came. They left everything where I'd been skinning and cutting in the barn. After the fire, and after he was sure the soldiers weren't coming back, Gerhard laid the meat on a smoldering log to cook. His hands were so badly burned that he could barely stand to touch anything, but he forced himself to do it.

We try to feed him, but he won't let us, no matter how much it still hurts to hold anything. He tires easily, and mostly wants to lie down and sleep. I feel his forehead and realize he has a fever. We sponge his sweaty face with wet rags.

I go out by myself into the forest to search for our rabbit traps, but I'm quickly lost on my own. Pieta and I try to start a fire with Gerhard's flint and knife but can't make a spark. He rouses himself and fumbles with the flint and knife but can't do any better. He throws them across the barn in frustration. We wrap him in all the blankets so he'll be warm enough to sleep. Pieta and I sit around and watch him, not knowing what else to do except chew on straw, like cows chewing their cud. I think about milk. Sweet, rich, creamy milk from Opa's dairy cows. He called them Milk Boats. I think about cheeses. And sausages. I chew harder on a mouthful of straw. Pieta laughs at me. She actually laughs. I look at her, chewing her straw, too, and I say, "Hello, cow," and I laugh, too, because what else is there to do?

Pieta moos.

We look through every corner of the barn for something, for anything that we can eat or use to catch something to eat. Anything besides straw. The pump still works next to the shell of the burned-out farmhouse, and we fill our bellies by drinking as much as we can. Pieta kicks an empty can and realizes there is something inside. She picks it up and brings it back to the cold barn, but it's too dark to see. I stick my fingers inside, careful not to scrape the jagged edges where it's been opened, and feel something squishy. I sniff and it smells rancid.

"Taste it," Pieta says anyway. She can smell it, too, and wrinkles her nose. "Maybe it's something the soldiers had to eat."

I'm pretty sure it's some kind of potted meat. I try it and it's as awful as I fear. But it doesn't make me vomit, so I eat some more. There's not much. I hold it out to Pieta and she tries it. We scrape as much as we can and share it with Gerhard. Then we cut the can open down the sides with the knife and lick out what little remains. Pieta keeps rubbing her fingers over the inside of the can, keeps sucking on her fingers, as if she's found hidden molecules of the potted meat juice.

We all feel sick that night when we bundle ourselves back up to sleep, buried together under the blankets and as much straw as we can find and pile on top of us. Pieta says she thinks she's going to throw up, but in the end she doesn't, and that's how we have our first meal of any kind since the rabbit.

In scouring the barn, I find more wire. That's the good news. Tomorrow I'll set a new trap and hope we can catch a rabbit. The bad news is we have nothing to start a fire, and I don't know how we'll cook it and eat it. I tell Pieta—and try to convince myself—that that's a problem we'll figure out in the morning.

Gerhard is still sleeping his feverish sleep when the new day dawns. Pieta wants to stay with him, but I insist that she comes with me when I venture out to set the new rabbit snare. We have to take off our mittens to twist the wires into place and at just the right height. I make Pieta set the trap while I give her instructions. She keeps fumbling everything with her frozen fingers, but I won't let her quit until she's done it right.

"Now can we go back?" she asks, blowing on her pink hands. I peel bark off a fir tree for us to chew.

"We should bring as many sticks as we can carry," I tell her. "And tonight, after it's dark, we'll try again to build a fire. Just a small one in the barn. If no one can see the smoke, it should be safe."

Pieta shakes her head.

"What?" I ask her.

But then I remember. It's this gnawing hunger, I think, making me fuzzy. Of course we still have no way to make a fire, even if we gather all the sticks and logs and fallen trees in the whole Memel Forest.

CHAPTER 44
PIETA

Mama took us to church on Sundays where we sat in the hard pews and bowed our heads and said prayers. At home we said a prayer for Papa every night. We were told in school to pray for Hitler and Germany and winning the war, but Mama left those out. Mama said we should pray for others; we shouldn't pray for things. I worried that I was selfish because I sometimes prayed for things, anyway. I prayed for a fish of my own that I would keep in a glass bowl. I promised to feed him and take proper care of him. And I prayed for a dog, even though we weren't allowed to have a dog in the apartment, and even though Mama said there wasn't enough money that she earned sewing uniforms for another mouth to feed, even a tiny mouth of a fish or a dog or even a pet mouse, which I also prayed for but never got.

I think it might be all right if I pray for matches, even though matches are a thing. I hold my hands together tightly, squeezing my fingers also to warm them at night when Asta and Gerhard and I burrow under the blankets and coats and straw in the freezing barn. An owl has made its way into the rafters and is whooing in the night, and I forget my prayers for a minute and wonder if we could catch the owl, and if we could eat the owl if we caught it. But, once again, the fire . . .

So I return to my prayer and ask again for matches, for any way to start a fire to make us warm and to cook the rabbit and the owl if we were to catch them, and anything else we could find to eat. Maybe there are mice scurrying around in the barn where we can't see them. Because why else would the owl have come in here? I am excited, thinking about that, and I whisper it to Asta, worried that if I am too loud my voice might wake up poor Gerhard and also frighten off the owl and the mice and even the rabbits in the Memel Forest, and the hares, which I explained to Asta are not the same as rabbits, though most people think they are.

I used to worry about the animals, and I didn't want to eat them, but now I am different. I am so hungry all the time, I can only think about what will fill my stomach besides snow and bark and straw and the juice and scraps from a tin of old potted meat.

Gerhard says there is another farm five miles away and maybe we can find something there. He says he will get up and show us, but even though his fever is gone, he is still too weak and we make him stay. His burned hands have healed some, but his fingers are bent and look like claws. He tries to straighten them, but it hurts too much.

"Their names are the Beckers," he says. "Maybe the soldiers have missed them and haven't burned down their farmhouse. But be careful on the road."

"I know, I know," Asta says. "Any sign of soldiers, hide right away."

"What if they are *our* soldiers?" I ask.

Gerhard shakes his head. "They won't be."

Asta and I walk and walk and walk down the lane from the farm and are already tired by the time we reach the road. Almost as soon as we get there, we hear trucks, and we run into the trees for cover just in time as a small convoy passes. There are red stars on the doors. After the trucks, there are men on horses, and horses pulling carts filled with things hidden under canvas, and horses pulling a cannon, and men on foot.

Once they've passed, we continue until we find what looks like another farm road and we follow it a long, long way until it, too, ends at empty fields and an empty barn and another farmhouse that's been burned to the ground. My heart sinks. There can be no one here. Asta sighs. But we have to make sure.

"Stay here," Asta says when we reach the barn. "Let me look inside first." She leaves me and I do what she says. I stamp my feet on the cold ground to keep the feeling in my toes. I see a small, frozen pond and it makes me think of my ducks and ducklings back at Opa and Oma's farm, only there are no ducks or ducklings here. No animals of any kind. Maybe in the barn. Asta is gone a long time and finally I decide to follow her, but just as I am poking my head inside, she is in front of me pushing me back out, blocking me from seeing anything past her.

"Let's go," she says. "We have to leave now."

"But I'm tired," I say. "I want to sit down. Is there straw in the barn? Is it dry inside? Please, can we?"

But Asta says no. She seems angry. And frightened. Both.

"But look," she says, pulling something from her coat pocket. "I have this."

It's a silver smoking lighter like Opa had and he showed me how to use it one time. She thumbs the spark wheel against the flint and a tiny flame spurts out.

"Tonight in the barn," Asta says, pulling me back toward the farm road, "we'll make a fire and you and Gerhard can sit by it all night if you want."

Asta lets me hold the lighter. Just knowing that now we can start a fire is all it takes to make me happy.

CHAPTER 45
ASTA

I can't look at their faces. Some are lying face down and I am thankful for that small mercy. I hope they didn't have to see what was about to happen to them, though they must have known, even if they were ordered to turn away. Rats have come. They scurry off when I enter. I get sick from the smell but tie a rag over my mouth and nose and force myself to go through coat pockets. I find a lighter and can't believe my luck. I flick it and it burns. I shake it, and it's nearly full. The soldiers missed it. There is little else. A ribbon. A small, hand-sewn doll. The body is a sack filled with sand. The arms and legs are pieces of twisted cloth. Another piece of cloth covers something hard—the head. There is a face painted on. It is a potato. I hesitate for a second. Pieta would love to have a doll. She lost the one she found on the Vistula Spit. Someone took it when she was in the hospital. But she would rather eat the potato more, no matter how small and dried up it is. I tear off the potato head and put it in my pocket and finish looking through the barn for anything we might use. But there is nothing else.

I return to the bodies. I close my eyes and fold my hands and try to say a prayer for them, but nothing comes out. I don't know why they were brought into the barn, or how long they were kept here, or why the Red Army soldiers did these terrible things to them and left them lying here. They must have been a family. The Beckers. Now—like Mama, like Oma and Opa and Rolf, like Monika and Herr Müller and Riki—they are gone. I don't even know their names. Just their unburied bodies remain, and I have to leave them where they are for someone else to find.

I only wonder how long I can keep Pieta from seeing these things. Not that she hasn't seen plenty all along. Too much. And I have seen too much as well.

· · · · · · · · · ·

There are more Red Army soldiers on the road, and we have to hide again and again on the way back to Gerhard's aunt and uncle's farm. By the time we reach the barn it's almost dark, and even darker inside, but he is sitting up and says he's feeling better. "I've been drinking water. And I heard you talk about how delicious the straw is here, so I had some of that, too."

I can't believe he's telling jokes. This morning I was worried that we might lose him to the fever. But there's no time for fooling around. "Let me see your burns," I tell him. "While we still have some light."

He grunts. Gerhard hates for anyone to touch his hands, but there's no choice. I unwrap the rags. The best I can say is the burned skin doesn't look any worse than it did this morning. He follows me to the pump so we can run cold water over his hands, which is painful and makes him cry. He tries his best to hide it, but it hurts too bad.

I pat his hands dry and then wrap them again. Pieta, meanwhile, has been getting everything ready for the fire and excitedly shows Gerhard the lighter.

He's not impressed. "You already have my flint and my steel knife blade," he says. "What did you need that for?"

"We couldn't make the sparks," I say. "And you can't do it with your hands the way they are. Anyway, you should thank us."

Pieta, grinning, has already flicked the lighter and lit a pile of straw under a tent of small sticks. Small flames soon turn into bigger ones, and warmer, and we crowd around the fire, exclaiming about how wonderful it is. Even Gerhard.

Not that we are about to forget what Opa taught us about fire safety. Especially inside a barn. We're careful to sweep all the extra straw away from the fire circle on the dirt floor, and we have a rusty bucket filled with water from the pump, just in case. Night wind still sneaks in through the burned end of the barn, but we'll worry about that later.

"It's wonderful," Pieta whispers, reaching her hands out until she's practically touching the flames. We've pried some half-burned timbers from what's left of the farmhouse—charred beams and parts of doors and window frames, and Pieta begs me to throw them on and make our fire just a little bigger. I know I shouldn't. We should keep the fire small. Not risk attracting attention with the smoke. But it feels so good to finally be warm after so many days hiding in the forest and trying to sleep in the cold barn. "Just this one time," I tell Pieta, and she smiles as if I've given her the best present ever, and I lay on a couple of larger pieces of wood and realize I'm crying with something like happiness as the fire dances higher and brighter and warmer and I can feel all my fingers and toes.

Gerhard, always practical, says we should close the doors on the side of the barn. "They still work, you know," he says. So I get up and do that, too.

Then, to their astonishment, I pull out the potato. When Pieta sees it, her eyes widen and she starts crying. Gerhard actually shouts "Hallelujah!"

I use one of the logs as a cutting board and divide up the potato, then lay the slices as close as I can to the fire so they'll cook but not burn. We stare at them, our mouths watering, barely able to contain ourselves. At one point Pieta reaches out, but I grab her hand. "Wait until they curl on the edges," I tell her. "Remember in the hospital? We stuck the potato peels to the potbelly stove and ate them when they fell off? That's how we knew they were cooked. So this is like that. Sort of."

But Pieta shakes her head. No. She doesn't remember. And why does it matter, anyway? "Here," I say, and hand her one of the potato slices. "But try to chew it slowly."

She gobbles it down so fast I think she might choke. We don't wait any longer after that. I count out the slices—one for her, one for Gerhard, one me. Two for her, two for Gerhard, two for me. Three. That's all there is. They're still mostly raw. Dry. Chewy. But we don't care. It's food and we eat.

· · · · · · · · · · ·

We find a blackened pot, partly melted, in the remains of the farmhouse. We snare another rabbit, and I make Pieta watch when I butcher it, cooking the meat on the ends of sticks we hold over the fire at night, searing the organs in the pan and eating those next, boiling the head and bones to make broth, cracking open the bones for the marrow. Everything takes a long time and leaves us exhausted, which I think is good because when we're not busy finding food, preparing the food, scavenging for sticks and logs, raking through the ashes of the burnt farmhouse, it's too easy for our minds to wander, too easy to slip into sadness and loneliness, too easy to miss Mama, and for Gerhard to miss his family, too. I know when it happens to Pieta. She stares off at nothing. Her eyes tear up, though she tries to hide it from me. She wakes up in the night sometimes, like Gerhard, and cries when she thinks I won't know. I pretend I'm still asleep, and that I just happen to roll over with my arm around her. I pretend I don't know when she buries her face against me and shudders through tearful breaths until she's too worn out to go on and drops back off into sleep.

During the day, we watch for Red Army soldiers returning up the farm road, or coming from the forest and across the fields like they did when Gerhard went out to greet them. We won't make that mistake again. We have our plans for what to grab and where to run and where in the forest to meet if we're separated. We have even found a small cave, really just a crawl space, beneath boulders jutting out from a hillside not far from the river. Gerhard remembered it—he used to play there, he says—and showed us one day. His hands continue to heal. We tie up a blanket filled with straw and drag it to the cave to cover the dirt. It smells musty and dank, but we have learned to make shelter wherever we can find it. Just in case.

We are even a little hopeful—for a few days, anyway.

"Do you think the war will be over soon?" Pieta asks.

"Why?" I say.

"If the war is over, maybe the Red Army soldiers will go back to their homes. And maybe we can go back to Opa and Oma's."

"No one will be at Opa and Oma's anymore," I remind her, but she doesn't want to believe me.

"You don't know that," she says. "You didn't see them the day of the hunt."

"Mama said," I tell her.

"But she didn't say," Pieta says. "Not exactly. Not *that*."

I let it go. Why not let Pieta think what she wants? Why not let her wish for things to be the way they once were? I still haven't told her about the records office in Königsberg and that we have no way to find Papa, if he's still even alive.

I only say that I hope the war does end soon, and the Soviets do go away. "And maybe everybody will come back on the ships. And maybe we can even go back home. Maybe they'll rebuild the whole city and it will be even more beautiful than it was before, and we'll see everyone again."

Gerhard listens but doesn't say anything.

Pieta almost seems happy again. "And Papa, too," she says.

"Of course," I lie. "And Papa, too."

CHAPTER 46
PIETA

I am the first to see them—three figures, young, but I can't tell how young from far away. They appear only for a moment at the edge of the forest, just long enough for me to rub my eyes and then look again to convince myself that I'm not imagining things. And then they're gone. It happens three or four times, at odd moments during the day. I tell Asta and Gerhard and they go out to look. They even tramp through the snow to search for tracks. But by the time they do that, it's snowing again.

"I think you're just seeing things," Asta says. "But it's good to keep watch just in case."

So that's what I do, until darkness sets in, and I have almost convinced myself that Asta must be right, because all the rest of the afternoon I haven't seen anyone—at the edge of the forest or anywhere. And, thankfully once again, no soldiers.

At night we hear the bombing again from far away, and we feel it, too, as we have most nights since coming here. Gerhard has decided it is from the Red Army siege of Königsberg, but I don't know what a siege is, so I have to ask.

"It means they must have surrounded the city," he explains. "And there is bombing until the German army surrenders. The soldiers who have passed here, taking all the animals and food and burning the houses, I think maybe they are part of the siege."

But that doesn't explain the three figures.

· · · · · · · · · ·

The next night, I'm sitting alone by the remains of the fire, unable to sleep, when they come to the barn. The oldest, a girl, is holding a smaller boy wrapped in a thick bundle of blankets. Another boy hides behind her. They stand quietly, blinking, just inside the door. I can see them faintly in what's left of the firelight. I gather my coat tighter around me, lay more wood on the fire so it blazes up again, and motion for them to come over. They move slowly, cautiously.

"It's all right," I whisper. I lift the pot that is filled with only water. We haven't had any rabbit or even bone broth for two days. The water is all I can offer them. And the warmth of the fire.

They sit as close as they can to the flames and pull off their mittens to toast their hands. The girl takes off the little boy's boots and rubs his feet one by one. They are almost black. He sobs in pain, and that wakes Asta and Gerhard. I hear them sit up suddenly in the dark loft.

"Who is it?" Asta demands.

"It's the ones I saw," I tell them.

I turn to the girl. "Was it you hiding in the forest?"

She nods. The little boy keeps crying. His feet must hurt terribly. I don't understand why they are black. The other boy takes off his own mittens and boots and rubs his own fingers and toes. He bites his lip, but he starts crying, too.

Asta helps Gerhard climb down the ladder from the loft. He still can't use his hands for much. Asta joins the circle and introduces us to the others. They give their names in return: Christel, the oldest, then Willy, and finally little Max. Asta takes Willy's hands in hers and rubs them gently, and then his feet, and then his hands again, back and forth, until he stops crying. I think he must have been in pain like Max, only not as bad.

Max begs his sister to stop. "It hurts. It hurts." He can only say this over and over. Christel looks at Asta, as if she'll know what to do. People always think this of Asta. I always think this of Asta. But she says she doesn't know what to do for the little boy. Gerhard is the one who answers.

"It's frostbite," he says. "It has become gangrene. I'm sorry."

For hours we take turns gently rubbing the swollen feet, but the color never changes from the hideous blackened flesh and the circulation never returns. Max finally stops crying deep in the night and he stops breathing, too. Willy, his boots and mittens back on his pink feet and hands, sleeps next to the fire. We wrap him in blankets. I stay next to him so if he wakes up, he won't be alone. At sunrise, Asta and Christel carry Max out of the barn and lay him inside a small, empty shed the Red Army soldiers forgot to burn.

CHAPTER 47
ASTA

We have a service that afternoon for Max. Christel says they have always called him Zucker because he loved candy so much. He just turned three.

Pieta sings a lullaby in her small, quiet voice. With the winter wind blowing, we have to lean forward and strain to hear her. But I am proud of her anyway for doing it. Gerhard mumbles the Lord's Prayer. Willy tells a story about a time that Zucker stole a bar of chocolate and shoved it in his pocket. It melted before he could sneak away and eat it. They found him later, hiding in some bushes with his pants off and turned inside out so he could lick the melted chocolate out of his pocket.

We all hold hands in silence for a few minutes, and then I close the shed door, leaving Zucker alone there on the frozen ground. We won't be able to bury him until the earth thaws in spring.

Afterward, we sit by the fire back in the barn. Christel and Willy are the same ages as me and Pieta, and they are from Tilsit. Christel tells me these things when I ask, but then she's silent again. Willy seems to have used up all his words telling the story about the chocolate. I'm not sure if I should keep asking questions or leave them alone with their grief. And anyway, we have to find food. We always have to find food. I'm sad that they have lost their little brother, but I'm already worried about having two more mouths to feed. But when I stand up to go, Christel stops me.

"Do you know Tilsit?" she asks.

I nod. "Of course. Where they make the cheese. It's north from here."

"I don't like the cheese," she says. "But I would eat anything right now. We haven't had anything to eat for a long time."

Gerhard says why doesn't he take Willy to check on the rabbit traps—he says Willy can be his hands—and off they go.

Christel is eager to talk once they leave. "Planes bombed our town," she says. "Many tried to leave. More planes came and shot them on the road. Mama said we should stay because if we left, how would Papa know where we are when he comes back from the war? After three days hiding in the house, Mama had to go find food. Then the planes came again and bombed the town and Mama never returned. When the Red Army arrived a few days later, there was panic everywhere. I knew it wasn't safe to stay. All I could think to do was try to follow the river. We spent two weeks hiding in the forest. We saw another village, but there were Red Army soldiers everywhere, so we kept going. And then we saw this place. And you. We had to be sure it was safe. That you were safe. But we waited too long. Zucker kept complaining about his feet. I should have done something before."

I tell Christel that she couldn't have known what would happen. It wasn't her fault. Zucker was just too little. It was too cold and too hard.

All the things you say to someone. All the things that never help.

Pieta does better. She listens and nods and reaches out to squeeze and hold Christel's hand.

· · · · · · · · · · ·

The sun comes out and the snow melts quickly. The fields are still all stubble, but here and there in the days that follow we see green shoots poking up, though just when I think it may be an early spring, the snow comes again and buries it all.

More children come to the farm on the heels of Christel and Willy, looking for somewhere, anywhere, to sleep at night. Looking for something, anything, to eat. If they see a green shoot, they will pull it up and eat it, no matter what it is. They're all starving.

They mostly come from the villages nearby, orphaned by the Red Army. Their stomachs are distended, but we don't know what to do for them. Some sit like statues no matter how we try to rouse them, no matter how much water we give them to drink, or snow to eat, or bark to suck on and chew. Their teeth are falling out. Their gums bleed. Their eyes glaze over. A few lie down and never get up. We carry them to the shed with Zucker.

Most pass through before we even learn their names. They stay for the night, but when they realize we don't have food to share, they leave. We don't know where they're going. They don't know where they're going, either. Some have stories about soldiers who shot at them for no reason. Like rats in a barn. Some of them say if you hang around the Red Army camps and do work for them, they'll reward you with a crust of bread, an apple core, a rind of sausage. Then they'll chase you away. But how can both be true at the same time?

Pieta becomes mother to the littlest children, watching after them while their older brothers and sisters look for food. I don't know what has come over her, but she has endless patience for these children. She sits for hours with them in her lap, singing them songs, playing little games, sweeping away straw and drawing with sticks in the dirt—pictures of tidy little houses with trees and flowers and smoke coming out of the chimneys. The children beg her to draw pictures of food and she does that, too: potatoes and carrots and apples and chickens and hams and sausages. She tells them stories.

Gerhard and Willy stay busy setting and checking the rabbit traps. They also try to snare birds but only manage to catch a few small ones that are mostly just feathers and bones. They hike through the forest to the river, which is still frozen, and try their hands—or Willy's hands—at ice fishing from the bank.

I go out every day with Christel to hunt for mushrooms and berries and anything green and edible, though it's still too early in the year to find much of anything. Once the ground is soft enough, we dig a hole in the forest, taking turns with the one shovel we have found in the barn. Using sticks. Using our hands. We cover it as best we can and then hope for a wild boar to fall in, or even a deer.

But instead of trapping a wild boar or a deer, we find a horse—not in the forest but out on the road. It has died there, and the Red Army soldiers have rolled it off to the side and into a ditch.

Two of the new boys, Sammy and Franz, tell us about it when they show up at the barn, a week after Christel and Willy and Zucker.

"We tried to eat some, but it was too hard to pull any of the meat off," says Sammy, who is fifteen but looks as though he could already be serving in the army. He is a head and shoulders taller than Franz, but it's Franz who does most of the talking.

"We will show it to you," he says, "but you have to agree that most of the meat belongs to us. In exchange for your knife, we will let you have some, too." He adjusts his glasses, as if he is an accountant adding and subtracting figures. One of the lenses is missing. The other is cracked.

Gerhard says no. "I'll butcher the meat. And you can have the biggest share. But I keep the knife."

Franz grumbles. Sammy stomps his feet. He is older than, us, too, but Gerhard won't budge. I stand next to him. And Christel and Willy stand with us, too. We still seem small in comparison to the teenagers. But they eventually give in.

For the next three nights, everyone feasts, and everyone is happy. Even Franz and Sammy, though they sleep closest to the fire and want to keep it burning all the time, even during the day, when we're worried that someone might see the smoke. But they insist, and they are pleasant enough otherwise, so we give in. There are ten of us now at the barn. We roast the meat on sticks, boil the bones for broth, cook everything we can think of to cook until the meat goes rancid and a few of the children become sick. Pieta has been mothering two of them, but once the horsemeat is gone, their older sisters and brothers take them and leave in their never-ending search for food.

CHAPTER 48
PIETA

For the next few weeks, as the snow melts for good, Franz and Sammy come and go, but Christel and Willy stay with us at the barn. I tell Asta that I think Willy is also a barnacle—to Gerhard. "The Barnacle's Barnacle!"

She laughs, then says, "I thought you weren't going to call him that anymore."

"Only just this one last time," I say. "I promise."

Gerhard's hands are now recovered from the burns, and he and Willy spend much of their time in the forest and at the river's edge. The Memel is wide there, too wide to cross, and running too fast now that the ice is breaking up—even if there was a boat. And we don't know what we would find there, even if we ever did manage a way into Lithuania. Gerhard says the Forest Brothers are fighting the communists over there, too, and we have to wonder if it can be safe for us anywhere.

Asta and Christel are also a team, like Gerhard and Willy—foraging in the fields and through the forest. I'm the only one who is alone. The children I was watching have left, so I busy myself cleaning the barn, bringing in wood for the fire, rolling logs into place for us to sit, scouring the burnt pots we've been using for cooking and for carrying water. In the loft, I plump up the straw and tuck it under blankets to make softer bedding.

I don't like Franz and Sammy, and whenever they are around, I try to make myself invisible. I go outside. I busy myself even more. I wash my hair under the freezing well water and try to comb out the lice that is now plaguing us all, making our scalps itch and keeping us awake at night.

"You, girl," Franz barks at me. "More sticks for this fire, yeah?" He smiles at me, but it's not a nice smile. He can't even be bothered to know my name. I complain about him to Asta, but she just says they'll leave again soon enough, and one of these times they won't come back.

"We can't make them go," she says.

"Why not?" I ask. "Gerhard doesn't like them, either."

"Because they need a place to stay, too. Just like us." She shrugs. "And they're bigger than us. They might be able to protect us if someone else comes."

I tell her I don't think those two would protect us. "They would just run away. And besides, Gerhard is the only one with a knife."

"It will be okay," Asta says, and that means she doesn't want to talk about it anymore.

A few days later, with no luck for a while catching rabbits or birds or fish, Gerhard and Willy agree to go with Franz and Sammy to one of the villages a few kilometers away. When they get there, they watch for a long time, hidden in the trees. The Red Army soldiers have taken over the houses, the stores, the barns, everything. They throw their trash in a great pile on the edge of the village. At dusk, when no one is around, the boys cross the clearing to look for food scraps. They can't believe what they find! Potato peels, apple cores, half-chewed bones. They stuff as much as they can into their pockets and into their mouths. They hear voices coming and race back to safety in the woods and make their stumbling way back to the barn.

That night, sitting next to the fire, they tell us of the adventure as we eat everything they have scavenged, even the bones. We gnaw on them like animals. With bricks from the farmhouse, we crack them open to even eat what's inside.

"Shouldn't we save some?" I ask.

"We'll go back tomorrow," Gerhard says. "The soldiers will keep eating, which means they'll keep throwing stuff away."

· · · · · · · · · · ·

At first it's just the boys, but soon we are all going to the village, though seven of us seems like too many. But I don't want to be left behind with so much food being tossed out by the soldiers, and neither do Asta and Christel. We wait just outside the village until it's almost dark, hugging the ground whenever the Red Army guards walk past, and then slip across the clearing to the garbage pit. There's never a lot, but everything we find is a feast for us. Twice we're almost caught, and Asta says we need to be more careful. She says we should only go every few days from now on.

Franz huffs. "I don't take orders from a girl," he says.

"Me either," says Sammy.

No one says anything back. Maybe in a different world they would be nice boys. But in this world, they care only about themselves and each other.

"Fine," Asta says. "Go whenever you want. But the rest of us will be more careful from now on."

We still can't believe our good fortune. Sometimes the food from the soldiers' garbage makes us ill, but we no longer have to forage in the forest and the fields so much and for so little. Gerhard and Willy continue to check the rabbit snares, and twice we're lucky there, too, though Franz and Sammy, as usual, take extra portions of the meat when it's cooked.

Gerhard is furious, but Asta tells him not to say anything.

· · · · · · · · · · ·

One afternoon when we're hiding outside the village, there is an accident out on the road. Another horse is hit by a Red Army truck. We watch from a distance as it struggles to get up. One of its legs is broken and it bellows in pain. I cover my hears, but I can still hear it. An officer pulls out his pistol and aims it at the horse's head. We hear the gunshot, and then another.

Instead of butchering the horse to eat it themselves or rolling it into a ditch to rot like the one Franz and Sammy found, they dig a pit next to the trash pile, drag the horse to the edge, and shove him inside. They pour out two large bags of white powder over the carcass. It looks like chalk dust.

As soon as the soldiers leave, Franz and Sammy slip out of their hiding places and start across the clearing. Franz whispers to Gerhard that he should come as well with his knife.

But Asta stops them. "We can't eat it," she says.

The boys stop. "What? Why? No!"

"The powder is quicklime," Asta says. "It's poison. They kept it in the outhouses at Opa and Oma's. Opa said it burns if you get it in your eyes or on your skin. It'll burn your throat, too, if you swallow it."

We go back to barn empty-handed. Franz and Sammy complain and complain. "We could have eaten it anyway," Franz says. "I don't know why we listened to you." He says this to Asta in an ugly voice.

That makes Gerhard mad. "Don't talk to Asta that way," he says, standing up.

Sammy stands up, too. He is much taller than Gerhard and easily pushes him down to the ground. Willy helps Gerhard up.

"That's enough," Asta says. "It's late. We're going up to the loft."

Nobody says anything else. Franz and Sammy stay behind to sleep by the fire as they always do. The others whisper among themselves in the loft. I only listen. "We have to do something," Christel says, "to make them go away." But no one can think of what. Asta can only say once again that they will eventually leave on their own and we'll have to put up with them until then.

In the morning, the fire has burned itself out and Franz and Sammy are gone. At first we're happy. Cold and stiff, busy restarting the fire, but happy. But then we realize they have taken our pots, which were all we had for cooking and carrying water. The lighter is gone, too. We hear Gerhard, still up in the loft, throwing straw and blankets. Cursing. I didn't realize he knew such language!

When he climbs down, he tells us the worst news of all: "They stole the knife."

It is as if someone died.

CHAPTER 49
ASTA

Three days later, on our way through the forest to look for food, we find them. They have made a camp not far from the Red Army village. They must have come back for the horsemeat. Franz is lying on the ground next to their fire. It has burned out. The coals are cold to the touch. Sammy is wrapped in blankets under a lean-to they have made with sticks. He moans but doesn't open his eyes. The pots are there. The lighter. The knife. Everything.

They cooked and ate the poisoned meat. Some is still left on a log near the fire. Even the forest animals have left it alone. Gerhard and Willy take the pots and go for water from the river. Christel and Pieta and I make Sammy as comfortable as we can. He is feverish, and when he speaks it is all nonsense. We carry Franz into the woods and cover him with branches and stones.

By the time Gerhard and Willy return with the water, it's already too late for Sammy. It was probably too late for him no matter what we did.

"They are too heavy to carry," Gerhard says. "We will have to leave them here."

Christel objects. "We can't just leave them. We have to bury them."

Pieta says we should forgive for them, even though they were mean to us, and even though they stole our things. "They lost their families, too," she says.

So we do. And we come back the next day with the shovel, to bury them in the soft earth, and wooden crosses Pieta made them last night with their names written in coal. She places them on the graves and says a quiet prayer.

· · · · · · · · · · ·

I don't know how they hear about us, these three new children who come a few days later. Mama called them waifs when we were in Königsberg, the ones without parents, the ones begging in the street. Back then, the waifs would be taken to an orphanage. Mama assured me of this when I worried about them. They would be clothed and fed. They would have beds to sleep in with clean sheets and warm blankets and a warm fire in the stove.

Now we are the ones who take care of them. Tinka is the oldest. She is seven. The little ones are Ilsa and Ada. Ilsa is four and Ada is three. We share our beds and blankets with them in the hay loft. At night, we build our fire in the barn and everyone circles around it, inching in as closely as they can. Pieta takes them under her wings.

I don't know how we have survived this long. We are all so thin now, like skeletons. Our clothes are torn and ragged and hardly clothes at all. More like scraps of cloth we tie around ourselves the best we can, in layers. We never wash. Maybe as spring warms the river, and maybe if we can find a shallow beach, we will be able to wade there and bathe ourselves and wash our clothes. Lay everything out in the sun to dry. Feel clean for once.

We go to other villages near us in our search for food and they are mostly empty, too. The fathers and children and grandmothers and grandfathers have all gone. The ones still there work for the Red Army soldiers. A handful of older girls and women Mama's age. We rarely see any old people anywhere. Sometimes we see other children in the forest who are afraid of us. Afraid of everyone. They run away. We know they won't last long on their own, even now that the winter has passed.

Then there are the others, another wave of children who find us, like Tinka and Ilsa and Ada. They think we have food and will feed them, and sometimes they're grateful for whatever we can give them, and sometimes they're disappointed, and even angry. We share what we have. That's all we can do. Most of them leave after a few days, looking for something better. Looking, I think, for something they are not likely to find.

Their stories are all different and all much the same—and much the same as ours in many ways. Their fathers are gone to the war. Their older brothers, too, even the teenagers. Their villages were bombed. Their houses were destroyed. Their families were killed. The Red Army came. Their families fled, but the Soviet soldiers caught them. Or they stayed to surrender and the Soviet soldiers threw them out of their homes. Or their mothers and grandparents were taken into the woods and never came back. Or their mothers and grandparents starved and the children starved, too. Or their mothers and grandparents became ill and there was no one to save them. Or the children were given away to another family, but that family couldn't care for them, either. Or they became separated in the chaos of the war and the evacuation and couldn't find their families again. Or they don't remember how they came to be on their own.

They, too, have been surviving on garbage, on handouts, on anything they can put in their mouths. They, too, have become ill. Have frozen night after night sleeping wherever they can, sometimes in ditches, sometimes next to their brother or their sister who was alive when they lay down but who was no longer alive when they woke.

• • • • • • • • • •

Christel and I make our way together through the forest one day to the river's edge and look across. The boys are off checking their traps. Pieta stays with the children. We have brought wire for fishing but can only spear bugs on the ends. Mostly the bait just falls off, or the fish steal the bugs without biting down on the wire. We don't catch anything. The body of a cow floats by and I have to stop Christel from wading into the river to try to get it. She would drown. The meat is probably bad, anyway.

Two new boys emerge from the forest behind us. They are small and seem harmless.

"You're never going to catch anything," one of them says. He wears a funny cap with feathers stuck in the band. Stringy blond hair juts out over his ears. "Not without a hook and real bait."

I hold up my length of wire. "I made a hook at the end," I tell them. "See? And I stuck a fly on it."

The other boy laughs. "I don't see a fly."

"That's probably because a fish ate it," Christel says.

"So where's the fish?" the boy asks. He has a knit cap pulled tightly down on his head. He doesn't seem to have any hair or eyebrows.

Christel and I both shrug. "It got away."

"Do you have any food?" the first boy asks.

We shake our heads, though it's not exactly true. We have both been saving a handful of unripe berries in our pockets to eat later.

"Sorry," I say.

It's their turn to shrug. "That's okay," the second boy says. "We're going across the river anyway. There's food over there."

"In Lithuania?" Christel asks, though of course that's where. It's the only place on the other side of the Memel River.

"How?" I ask.

"There is a railroad bridge," the boy tells us, pointing upriver. "Two hours from here. Maybe three hours. I don't know. We make hamster runs to the villages over there. The soldiers here hate every-one who is German. Over there, the Lithuanian people, they hate the Soviets just as much because they wish they were free from the Soviets. There hasn't been so much war there. Only some. But not like here. Some of them will give us food."

"You ride the train?" I ask, surprised. "Who has tickets for a train?"

He laughs at me. Christel and I look at each other. He wipes his runny nose, this boy, and introduces himself. His name is Arno, and I think he may be my age, but everyone looks both younger and older at the same time. Younger because we are all so thin and small. Older because our bones show through like old people's faces. The hat is too big for him.

"You wait at a curve in the tracks for the freight train to slow down," Arno says. "Sometimes they even have to stop before the bridge to let another train cross first. You climb onto the side and stand on a ledge, a running board, and you hold on until you're across the river. And then you jump off. You bring your begging sack. You never, ever, ever speak German to the people there. You just look at them and open your sack and if they speak to you, you only nod. That's all. Sometimes they yell at you. Sometimes they might even threaten you with a knife or a gun. Then you have to run away. But sometimes you get food. Sometimes you get old clothes. Or a blanket. Once I got some old shoes. These shoes."

He shows me his feet. He's wearing shoes for a grown man, with rags stuffed all around the insides to hold them in place.

The boy's friend takes off his knit cap, and sure enough, he has no hair at all anywhere on his head. Including the eyebrows. He says his name is Josef, and he laughs. "Arno didn't get those shoes like that," Josef tells us. "He stole them. They chased us in that village. Now we can never go back. Now it's probably not safe for any of us to go there anymore."

"You can come with us tomorrow," Arno says. "Maybe we'll have better luck to have girls with us. We are camping not far from here." He gestures vaguely into the forest.

Before I can answer, Christel does. She says, "We have a barn. You can stay the night and we will go with you in the morning."

CHAPTER 50
PIETA

The next morning, Gerhard and Willy want to go across the river, but Asta has other ideas.

"There are already two boys," she says, pointing to Arno and Josef, who are warming themselves by the fire.

"So?" Gerhard says.

Asta puts her arm around Christel's shoulders. "Arno said it would be better to have girls go with them so it's not a gang of boys knocking on people's doors. People might be worried if they see a gang of only boys."

Gerhard argues back—"Why should Arno or anybody else get to say who goes?"—while Willy looks on. I can tell that he's not sure he wants to go so far away and jump on a train and cross the river and beg for food in another country where they speak another language. None of us has ever been out of East

Prussia before. All of it sounds scary and dangerous.

Arno interrupts from the fire to point out that it's already starting to get light out and there's not much time to get to the train.

In the end, Asta has them draw straws to see who goes. "The shortest straw stays here," she says. I'm not sure how she does it, but she somehow makes sure that Gerhard loses. He protests, but he's not sure how she did it, either. Asta can be tricky that way.

She turns to me. "I promise we will come back as soon as we can," she says. "We will bring as much food as we can carry. And maybe some clothes."

Gerhard pouts, but Willy looks relieved. Christel pulls on her own knit cap and a long, ragged scarf that she tucks inside her coat. Asta does the same. They follow Arno and Josef outside, and I go with them.

We pause at the edge of the field while the two boys march ahead. "Are you sure you can trust them?" I ask. "They won't be like Franz and Sammy?"

"I think so," Asta says. She looks at Christel, who only shrugs. "We have to do something. We need food."

"But in the fields things are starting to grow," I say. "Every day now that the snow is gone. We can find things to eat here."

Asta nods. "That will be good for the children to do. The little ones. You have the shovel. And they can use their sticks. They can dig up some of the shoots."

Christel tugs at Asta's sleeve. "We have to catch the boys," she says. "We have to go. The sun is already over the trees. Look."

And she's right. The dull sun has crested the tree line. Already it's warmer in the daylight. Or maybe I only convince myself of that in my mind. I tuck my hands under my arms. I follow Asta and Christel halfway across the still-frozen field before I stop and watch as they continue. At the edge of the forest, Asta turns and waves to me, then they disappear.

I run after them. I start to shout for them to stop, to come back, but I trip on the stubble and fall hard to the ground. I sit and hug myself and rock back and forth. My breath forms a cloud that hangs in the air. I tell myself that of course they will return. Of course Asta will never leave me. Never for very long. I am all the family she has, and she is all the family I have.

CHAPTER 51
ASTA

By the time we find the railroad bridge, we're exhausted. We stay hidden in the forest as a long line of Red Army soldiers passes on a muddy road. There are guardhouses on both sides of the tracks on the East Prussia side of the bridge, and a fence we'll have to crawl under to get to the train when it comes. The sun disappears behind clouds and we shiver. The hours we spent making our way through the forest left us wet all over as we waded through streams, squeezed through narrow passages between boulders, brushed against the wet trunks of trees and saplings, ducked under limbs still heavy with melting ice and snow.

We all keep our eyes glued on the nearby guardhouses. We need to stay as close as we can to the tracks so we can run to catch the train. The guards come out and stand at attention when the Red Army soldiers pass on the road, but afterward, they go back inside.

Smoke rises from a stovepipe that juts out of the roof of each hut. We pray that the guards stay where it's warm when it's time for us to move.

We hear the train before it arrives, the same whistle we've heard on trains all our lives, and yet today it sounds different. Maybe because the world is so different than the one from before. As soon as it pulls into sight and slows in its approach to the bridge, Josef says, "Now!" and we go, Christel and I following the boys out of the woods, through a ditch. Arno holds two wires far enough apart that we can climb, and soon we're crouching next to the track, all four of us with our begging sacks, flattening ourselves to the ground. The train draws closer. The guardhouse door stays closed. The whistle blows again. The door opens and a guard leans halfway out and waves at the conductor. The conductor waves back. The guard retreats.

And suddenly we're up and running beside the train. Arno and Josef step onto the running board as easily as if it was someone's front porch and nothing at all to it. Christel jumps up, too, and they grab her. I'm still running as the engine starts over the bridge, and only at the last second do I make it. They're together on the freight car in front of me, but I can't think about that. I have a death grip on a hand rung and I press my face against the icy steel of the side of the car. At first I look down and can see through slats in the bridge the black water churning ten meters below with chunks of ice and logs and other floating debris racing along in the fast-moving current. I close my eyes. I'm afraid to keep looking. The train trembles and rattles and sways over the wooden bridge. Sparks fly off the tracks from under the wheels. I can't feel my hands. They're numb from holding on so tightly. My wet boots feel as though they're slipping and I could fall from the train at any time—fall into the Memel River and drown.

But then before I know it, we're across on the other side and Christel is yelling at me to jump, and Arno and Josef are yelling, too: "Jump, Asta! Jump!" And without looking I let go and throw myself off the train, landing hard on my back, knocking all the breath out of me, leaving me stunned, gasping, frantic, flailing.

Christel is kneeling over me. She takes my hand. She tells me to breathe, breathe. The boys are behind her, laughing. Christel says something to them, something in her angry voice, but they keep laughing. And then they, too, kneel down and help me sit up. I shudder through a breath and then another and then another, and absurdly, I, too, am laughing and also crying at the same time. But there's no time for anything. They drag me to my feet and tell me to come on, we can't stay here, the guards might follow us from the other side of the river. There might be soldiers here as well. And we're stumbling away from the tracks, and the train is rumbling out of sight, and we find our way to a road that the boys say will take us to the first village.

"The begging isn't good there," Josef says. "Too close to the tracks."

The Lithuania side of the river looks the same as the East Prussia side. The same trees, the same muddy roads, the same brick and thatched-roof farmhouses, the same towering barns and grain silos. The first village is a crossroads, a collection of small shops. A school and two churches. Small white houses with steep roofs and fences. A cow and a goat and chickens. Horse carts and wagons.

The difference is there's no war. Nothing bombed or burned. No bodies lying unburied in the ditches. No soldiers in the streets.

"You go to the first house," Josef says, pushing me ahead of him. "Remember, don't speak in German. Only say this in Lithuanian: Prasome padeti."

But I'm afraid. "Why can't we all go together?"

"Too many," Arno says. "If it's just one, and just a girl, they are more likely to give something. They take pity."

Christel asks, "What does it mean, *Prasome padeti*?"

Josef answers. "It means 'Please help.'"

I repeat it over and over in my mind as I go to the cottage. As soon as I touch the gate to open it, a black dog emerges from under the steps and snarls and runs toward me. Only the chain on his collar stops him. I am already racing back across the road to the others, who have been watching, half-hidden in the trees. An old woman comes out of the cottage. She shouts at the dog. Then she shakes her fist at us and shouts again. She looks up and down the street. No one else is out, though it's now the middle of the day.

She pulls something from a pocket in her apron and tosses it over the fence and into the road, then she goes back inside, taking the black dog with her.

As soon as she's gone, we sneak over to inspect. It is half a carrot. Arno grabs it and we run back across the road to our hiding place. While we watch, salivating, he very carefully breaks it into four pieces and hands one to each of us. I try to savor mine, try to force myself to chew slowly, but it's no use. My stomach has been empty for so long. I swallow and then despair that my bite of carrot is already gone.

CHAPTER 52
PIETA

The earth is still too frozen, and the tips of the green shoots are too tiny, so we give up after an hour scouring the fields. Tinka collects a small handful, but not enough to bother cooking. She shares with her sisters, who immediately stuff the leaves into their mouths. Gerhard whittles pointed sticks for us to catch frogs, but if there are any in the woods, they are much better at hiding than we are at finding them. At midday, the little kids go back to eating bark and new tree leaves and snow. Ada, the youngest, I find in a corner of the barn licking dirt from her hands.

Gerhard and Willy come back from the forest once again with no rabbits, no hares, no anything. For awhile they sit in the barn, staring at nothing. Gerhard says to no one in particular that he should have gone across the river anyway, no matter what Asta said. And no matter who picked the longest straw.

"She cheated, anyway," he says.

I shouldn't say anything back but it slips out: "Probably."

Gerhard sits up and scowls. "I *knew* it!" He tries to sound angry, but I can tell he's not really. He just likes it that I told him he was right to be suspicious of Asta whenever she plays a game.

"Maybe tomorrow we'll go," he says to Willy and me. Willy says, "Okay," but not in a way that I believe he really wants to.

Gerhard says they're going to go fishing today instead. Even though Asta and Christel weren't able to catch anything. "But I bet we will."

They try to weave fishing lines from loose threads, but they only succeed in tearing bigger holes in their already-torn coats. They'll have to practically hang over the water to get their lines in, but Gerhard ties wire hooks on the end and says they're going to do it anyway. I decide to take Tinka and Ilsa and Ada and go with them to watch. We don't have anything else to do, and I don't want Ada eating any more dirt. That can't be good for you.

We're half an hour into our hike to the river when we hear a snuffling in the brush ahead. We stop suddenly. The little girls cling to me and Tinka. The boys grip their fishing poles and point the sharp ends forward. Gerhard takes out his knife. There is more snuffling, louder now, and closer. Tinka whispers, "What is it?" but no one answers. We don't move. We hardly breathe. We wait until we finally see them—two wild boars with spiky fur and tusks, their heads bowed, their snouts inches from the ground.

Maybe if we stay still, they won't know we're here.

But the foolish boys ruin everything. They charge at the boars, yelling, waving their fishing poles, as if their skinny little spears could ever hurt a wild boar. The boars lift their heads, slowly, lazily, as if they're bored and wondering what's going on and who's bothering them now? And then they attack the boys.

The next thing I know, we're all running. I'm holding hands with the two little girls, dragging them with me while Tinka sprints ahead. We hide behind a copse of trees and then pull ourselves onto a low-hanging branch that sags with our weight. The boars chase the boys right past the trunk. Willy trips and falls underneath us. A boar rips a long tear in the back of his coat with his tusk, then jabs at his legs. We shout, pull branches and twigs and leaves, anything that will break off, and throw them down at the boar to distract him. And it works. The boar lifts his head to look at us, and then wanders off into the forest.

We help Willy climb up with us, Tinka and I doing most of the work. He's still so frightened that he's shaking. And that's not all. His pant leg is torn, and he's bleeding. I wrap my scarf around his leg and cinch it as tight as I can.

"Where's Gerhard?" he asks, trying to sound brave. "I should go look for him."

"He ran the other way," Tinka says, pointing through the woods.

"I saw him stabbing his stick at the other pig. You'd better just wait here with us."

It's turning into late afternoon, half an hour later, when we hear more rustling in the bushes, but this time it's not the boars. It's Gerhard. The girls and Willy cheer when he emerges and we see that he hasn't been hurt. Gerhard smiles as if he's won a great victory and holds his fishing pole over his head like a real spear. The tip might be a little red, or might just be a little wet.

"Did you kill it?" Willy asks, excited.

Gerhard shakes his head sadly. "No. I only poked him a little. But I did make him run away."

We climb down from the limb and make our way back to the barn. Willy is limping, but I think he might be putting on a show for Gerhard for sympathy. I hear Gerhard say how brave Willy was, and I can tell that makes him happy.

· · · · · · · · · · ·

Asta and Christel are still not home when darkness falls. We're all hungry and we all have stomach cramps. We were hoping they'd bring back food, especially since we haven't found any ourselves. Just an attack by the wild boars. In the dancing firelight, I try to teach the little girls how to write their letters with sticks in the dirt. To distract them from their hunger. And to distract myself. Tinka knows her letters already, of course. Gerhard and Willy don't care. Ilsa and Ada copy the ones I draw, but they are tired as always.

I end the lesson early and we climb up to the loft where we throw ourselves down on our straw beds under our rotting blankets, pressed together for warmth. The girls beg me to tuck them in the way their mother used to do. I tell them a story Mama used to read to Asta and me when we were little about a boy named Emil and his detective friends. Emil is robbed on a train by a thief who takes all his grandmother's money. He recruits other children to help him track down the robber. They have many adventures, I tell the girls. Adventures just like our adventure today.

"And you are Emil," Ilsa says. "And we are the detectives."

I smile when she says this. It is the first time I have smiled in a long time, and it feels strange on my face. "I wish I was clever like Emil," I say, and they fall all over themselves to assure me that I am. It isn't true, but I like hearing them say it.

And then I have tears on my face as I think about what they have lost, these sweet children.

CHAPTER 53
ASTA

After we share the carrot, Josef and Arno say we should separate, them and us. "When these villagers see us all together, they think we might do something. Steal something," Josef says. "You saw the look on that woman's face."

"But she gave us the carrot," Christel says.

"Like *we* were the dogs," says Arno.

"I don't care," Christel says back. "It was something to eat. I don't care where it came from, or how we got it."

Josef picks up his begging sack. "We go," he says, turning away from us with Arno. "You know your own way to the railroad bridge."

"Wait!" I call after him. And then I look around to make sure no one else is near. We are still standing next to the road at the outskirts of the village. "I thought we were together."

Arno shrugs. "Maybe girls aren't so good for begging," he says, and just like that they leave us.

Christel wants to go to the bridge and wait for the next train back. She calls the barn our home, as if we've lived there all our lives.

But I insist that we keep trying. We've eaten the only food we've been given, and we can't go back to Pieta and Willy and the others with nothing. Josef and Arno have moved on from the village, but I tell her we should try other places here first.

We don't get far.

Halfway down the street, past the carrot woman's house, is an open-air market—stalls selling produce, cider, apples, cuts of meat, fish and eels, eggs, live chickens in cages. We both gasp at the sight of it all. But the vendors see us as soon as we come near, before we can even ask for anything. A big man in a butcher's apron reaches under his stall and grabs a club. Women who are there shopping turn to watch as he storms toward us, shouting in Lithuanian, raising his club.

We run away as fast as we can. He doesn't stop and shake his fist and toss half a carrot over the fence. He keeps chasing us, still shouting, swinging his club, out of the village until we throw ourselves off the road and into a ditch where we duck and cower, and pray he doesn't see us.

• • • • • • • • • • •

We are too afraid to go back through the village, or anywhere near it. And we have run so long and so far, we aren't sure which way to go to find the railroad bridge. When we convince ourselves that the butcher is no longer around, we drag ourselves out of the ditch, but instead of returning to the road we go deeper into the forest, skirting the few remaining snow drifts, looking for any kind of shelter. The afternoon soon turns to dusk, dusk to twilight. The best shelter we can find after an hour of searching is a shallow depression in the matted forest floor where we cover ourselves with brush and hold onto each other for what warmth there is to share through the long, cold night. Christel can't stop trembling. I wrap my arms around her tighter, but it doesn't seem to help. We're both miserable. I barely sleep, worrying about Pieta and Gerhard and the others, worrying that something could happen to them and I won't be there to help. I have been with Pieta every night, even when she was in the hospital. All our lives, for as long as I can remember.

· · · · · · · · · · ·

Christel and I go the wrong way in the morning. The wrong road. The wrong country. We nervously approach the first farmhouse we come to, because what choice do we have? We're starving and thirsty and wet and tired and lost. Christel has been shivering all night and still hasn't been able to stop, even as the sun rises in a cloudless sky and I can already feel it warming my face, although it's early. I smell breakfast cooking inside the house and imagine large vats of porridge, skillets popping with hot oil and frying eggs and sausages, stacks of Pfannkuchen with syrup.

I step onto a low porch and brace myself, ready to run again if it's another man with a club. Just as I'm about to knock, I realize that Christel has disappeared from behind me. I look around but don't see her anywhere. I should leave, but the smell, the wonderful smell, won't let me go. So I rap lightly on the heavy oak door, so lightly I doubt anyone will hear. But maybe it's a test. If they do hear, they'll give me food.

The door opens to a Hausfrau and two small children, peeking out from behind her skirts.

I stumble to speak, to remember the words the boys taught me to say in Lithuanian, but nothing comes out.

The woman stares down at me. I look up at her, begging with my eyes. *Please, please*, I think. *Please give me anything.*

She waits but doesn't say anything, either. The children keep staring at me, wide-eyed. The woman lifts her hand and I flinch, but she doesn't hit me. She just sighs, and looks sad, and closes the door.

Christel finds me back on the road. She is smiling, and she has stopped shivering. She tries to say something, but her mouth is too full.

"Do you have food?" I ask her. She doesn't stop chewing. She can only nod. She pulls handfuls of wet corn and grain and eggshells and other slop from her soggy pockets. I cup my hands. She swallows some of what she's eating, enough to tell me:

"From the hog trough."

··········

The way back is much harder. We wait near the farm until dark and then sneak back to the trough for more food. Someone leaves a bucket in the barn and we use it to scoop out as much of the pigs' slop as we can carry. We steal a horse blanket, too.

Because it's already late, we have to spend another night in the Lithuanian forest, but at least we're able to wrap ourselves in the blanket this time, and at least we have something to eat. It's hard not devouring everything in the bucket. Christel says we should, and then go back to the hog farm once more to refill it when it's feeding time there. But I'm afraid we'll be caught and tell her no.

An old man in a cart points us in the direction of the railroad bridge the next day after we pantomime a train. It's frustrating not being able to speak the same language. The Memel River is the only thing that separates East Prussia from Lithuania physically. But the languages separate us even more. It seems like a miracle that I'm able to hop on the train once we get there, holding on with one hand while I keep my death grip on the slop bucket with the other. The train slows to a crawl on the East Prussia side and I'm able to step off without spilling much. Another miracle.

We scurry away and under the wire and into the safety of the forest, and only then sit and catch our breath.

CHAPTER 54
PIETA

By the time the sun is overhead, Willy's leg is infected and he has a fever. By nighttime, and still no Asta and still no Christel, he is delirious. He is calling for his sister. Gerhard paces nervously, wanting to do something to help. I tell him to bring more wood in for the fire. I have the girls bring wet cloths from the pump with cool water that I press to Willy's cheeks and forehead. Though it's cold in the evening, Gerhard and I take off Willy's jacket and his boots. His clothes are drenched with sweat. I hold his head in my lap. Gerhard and the girls sit close to the fire and look on anxiously. I don't know what to do. I don't know what to tell them. We don't have any medicine. There's no place to go. No grown-ups. No doctors. No hospitals. I feel helpless and lost without Asta. I know she always puts on a brave face for me, so I won't worry about things, and now I'm the one who has to do that—Gerhard and me—for Willy and the girls.

I tell Tinka and Ilsa and Ada they should climb into the hayloft and sleep, but they don't want to leave us, and I understand. When you have lost so much, you cling to what you have left as hard as you can. I wish Asta and Christel would come back. I can't bear to think that something might have happened to them across the river. Deep in the night I have a panicked feeling that I will never see Asta again. I can't catch my breath when it happens, only in shallow sips. The girls and Gerhard have fallen asleep, despite their best efforts to stay awake to keep a vigil for Willy. I want to cry, but I can't let myself. I have to be strong for them. I have to help Willy, even if holding him is the only thing for me to do.

And then, late the next afternoon, Asta and Christel are back, dragging open the barn door and exclaiming that they have brought food.

But as soon as Christel sees me holding Willy she cries out. She rushes over and takes my place. He opens his eyes for a second and I think he sees her and recognizes her, but then he falls asleep again. The fever continues. His leg is swollen and red and leaking the infection. "What happened?" she sobs. "Why is he like this?"

I'm too tired to answer. I've been awake with Willy all night and all day. Tinka tells her about the wild boar, the tusk, the wound that we thought was nothing.

Christel rocks her brother and whispers to him, and we leave them alone. Asta sets down a bucket filled with food, though I can't tell exactly what, and the girls and Gerhard and I crowd around it with her. There are soggy grains and corn and what looks like hay and eggshells but none of us care. Asta scoops out careful portions and we cup our hands into bowls for our shares and bury our faces in it, licking and chewing and swallowing every bit. It is foul and gross and hard to get down, but it's food.

Asta brings the bucket over next to the fire. She and Christel try to coax Willy to eat some, but it dribbles down his chin. Gerhard, who joins them, tries to tuck some of it back between Willy's lips, but nothing works. He can't swallow. He still burns with the fever.

Asta hands me the bucket. Tinka and Ilsa and Asta follow me and look at it hungrily. We've eaten our portions, but it's not enough. "We should try to save some for later," Asta says. "Cover it and put it somewhere that they can't reach."

I have a thousand questions about what happened across the river, but they'll have to wait. Asta kneels again next to Christel and wipes Willy's sweaty face. Soon, though, despite the fever, he is shivering. We cover him with more blankets and build up the fire even higher, even though it's dangerous to do that in the wooden barn. But Willy is shaking so hard now we're afraid he will break something.

Finally, after the fire is blazing again, he stops, and this time his sleep is peaceful, or the closest thing to peaceful there can be.

Another night passes in this way. I get the little girls up into the loft and tell them stories until they're asleep, then join Asta and Christel and Gerhard back at the fire with Willy.

· · · · · · · · · · ·

The next morning, I follow Asta out of the barn to the pump where she drinks so much I have to ask if she turned into a camel while they were gone and thinks she is in the desert. It's cool out, but not cold, and she sticks her head under the water and asks me to keep working the pump until most of her is drenched, even her ragged coat. We sit outside in the faint warmth of the early sun. She shakes her head and water flies off and I tell her now she doesn't look like a camel, she looks like a wet dog that's just come from the river.

Asta smiles. I know these are dumb things I'm saying, not even funny, but it's been so long since anything was truly funny. I can't even remember. But I'm still happy she smiles.

I ask about the bucket and she says Christel stole it.

"And the food?" I ask her. "And the blanket? Did she steal those, too?"

Asta nods. "Yes, we both did that. But the farm where it came from, they won't miss it. They won't know."

"Are you going back?" I ask, and Asta nods again. She says it was scary jumping on the train the first time, but easier coming back, even though she had to hold on to the side of the train with one hand and the bucket with her other hand.

"It was so heavy," she says. "My shoulder is sore from carrying it.

Christel and I tried to carry it together, and we could when we were walking in the road, but we had to take turns through the forest. The trail was too narrow."

"You were gone for so long," I say. "I was afraid for you."

Asta hugs me with her wet arm and leans her head and her dripping hair against me. "We just got lost and it took us another day to find our way back."

"But what about Josef and Arno?" I ask.

Asta shrugs. "They left us. They thought if they had girls knock on people's doors we would get more handouts, but then they had second thoughts." She laughs. "I wish they'd left sooner. When we were with them a woman gave us one carrot that we had to split four ways. Half of one carrot. Christel and I would have done better without them from the start."

"More carrot?" I say.

"Yes," she says. "More carrot."

CHAPTER 55
ASTA

I don't tell Pieta about the butcher who chased us from the village with his club. I don't tell her about spending the cold nights with a shivering Christel in the wet forest, or about the woman on the farm shutting the door in my face. I don't tell her everything about coming back later and stealing the bucket and fighting our way past the hogs to the trough.

I don't tell her the things that once would have made me ashamed I now do without regret. I don't tell her that if I hesitate it's not to decide if what I'm about to do is right or wrong, but only to watch and study and wait until I think I can get away with it without being caught.

And besides, we're all too worried now about Willy. Sometimes he is delirious, thrashing around with fever, and sometimes he's himself, just weak and tired. He wants Christel to be his nurse, but then he gets annoyed with her because she's his sister and he doesn't want her babying him. It's very complicated.

"I can't stand him sometimes," Christel tells me our second day back from across the river. "He was always such a spoiled little boy. I used to tell Mama this."

She stops herself. Christel never talks about her mother. She never mentions Zucker. I think she feels guilty when she loses patience with Willy.

For a few days, there is food. We finish the hog chow from the slop bucket, and then, as if we planned it that way, Gerhard catches a fat rabbit and we grill it for our dinner, taking care to use all the other parts in a broth, which is all Willy can eat, and all we eat as well for the next two days until it's gone.

The next time we cross the river, Gerhard insists on going with us. But Pieta is worried about being left alone for so long with Tinka, Ilsa, Ada, and Willy, even though he seems to be doing better.

Gerhard pulls out his knife. He looks at it long and hard, then sighs and hands it to Pieta. "You can keep this while we're gone. For protection. Just in case of anything."

I can't think that Pieta would be able to defend them with the knife, or with anything, but it seems to work. She smiles and holds it close to her, as if it's a magic talisman that can ward off evil spirits.

And so off we go again to hop the train back into Lithuania.

· · · · · · · · · · ·

Late in the afternoon, after walking for miles, and begging at farmhouses, and being turned away again and again and again, we come across a small farm where at first we think no one is home, but then we see a girl tending a small herd of cows in a pasture nearby. Gerhard waits, hiding in the woods, while Christel and I climb through a low fence and cross the field to the girl. She is sitting under a tree, hardly paying attention to the grazing cows. She has on long skirts and an apron and an old sweater and a kerchief over her blonde hair that someone has braided into perfect pigtails. And she is clean.

She sits up suddenly and seems startled to see is. This time I remember what Arno and Josef taught me to say: Prasome padeti. But maybe I mispronounce it because she just stares at me. So I say it again, as a question. "Prasome padeti?"

And for some reason that makes her laugh. We smile along, not knowing what else to do. She says something in Lithuanian, but I don't understand her, either. Christel tells her, in German, that we only speak German, and maybe she understands that. Or probably she just recognizes the language, and what it means about who we are and where we are from—and why we are there.

She pats the ground next to her and we sit, then she takes a cloth out of her rucksack and unfolds it to reveal what must be her lunch: black bread, cheese, a sausage, some sort of tart. She breaks off part of the bread and gives it to us. Then some of the cheese and a bite of the sausage. The rest she folds back in the cloth. I slip some in my pocket for Gerhard, and we eat quickly, nervous that someone else from the farm—someone older, the girl's parents—might show up and chase us off or take away what the girl has shared. But before we leave, she stops us and leads us over to one of the cows. A calf has been nursing and she gently pulls it away from its mother. Then she kneels beneath the cow, grasps one of the teats, and squeezes out a thin stream of milk into her mouth. She smiles, wipes her face, and gestures for us to take a turn.

Afterward, we thank her, and she seems to understand. She places her hand on her chest and says, "Lina." We repeat it and she nods. She points to us and raises her eyebrows as a question, and we say our names, too.

Christel and Gerhard and I sit in the woods for the rest of the afternoon. Gerhard eats the food I saved, and as it grows warmer, we lie down and fall asleep, not full, but no longer starving. I wake up first and scoot to the edge of the forest, just beyond the fenced-in pasture, and watch the girl, Lina, while I wait for Christel and Gerhard to wake up, too. Mostly she just sits and stares at the clouds some more, sometimes getting up to tend to the cows. When it's milking time, Lina has a switch that she flicks at their rumps to herd the cows back to the barn, careful to keep them to a path and out of the fields along the way.

Christel and Gerhard wake up and sit next to me. We watch Lina in silence, all of us transfixed.

"It's like a movie," Christel says after awhile. "A beautiful movie. Or like a fairy tale."

Eventually, in the fading light of afternoon, we find our way back to the hog farm, where the woman with the children turned us away, and where Christel filled her pockets with slop from the hog trough. By the time we get there, it's feeding time again. We have brought the stolen bucket with us and wait until we see our chance.

CHAPTER 56
PIETA

It is late, and Asta and the others haven't returned yet from across the river. I know that it's hard to make the trip in only one day, and so the earliest they will be back is tomorrow afternoon. I hope they have food. Willy is resting easy down by the fire and I am up in the loft, trying with Tinka to get the little ones to sleep. Earlier, I taught them how to braid the long spring grasses into little dolls, and we practiced their letters and numbers once again. Now, instead of me telling Ilsa and Ada stories, they're telling them to Tinka and me, though they're not very good at it. They only remember parts of stories from when they were littler and had their family, and they're never able to remember what happens next. Ilsa tries to tell us "Hansel and Gretel," but she and Ada argue about the brother and sister dropping breadcrumbs to mark their path through the woods. Why would anyone ever waste good food like that? And when Hansel and Gretel get to the witch's gingerbread and cake and candy house and start eating it, the girls get sidetracked listing all the things they are certain must have made up the house. Tinka, too: Bee sting cake and spaghetti ice cream and red berry pudding. Caramel-chocolate chews and marzipan and strudels.

I finally have to tell them to stop because they're making me miss all those things too much and it's upsetting us all. Ilsa never gets to the part where the witch comes back home with plans to cook and eat the children. Hansel and Gretel never push the witch into the stove and save themselves and find the witch's precious jewels and take them back to their father, the woodcutter, so they can live happily ever after.

• • • • • • • • • • •

Later I go and sit with Willy. He is so quiet. I think he's asleep, and still getting better. The infection had spread up his leg and had begun to smell, but it hasn't gotten any worse for a while. Lying here now, his face is pale but he isn't sweating from fever and he doesn't seem to be in as much pain as usual. Then he takes a sudden turn. Something is wrong. I only realize he has stopped breathing when I wipe his face with a cool cloth. I hold my fingers under his nose but feel no air. I press my hands on his chest, to see if it rises and falls the way it's supposed to, even a little, but there's nothing.

I don't understand how death happens. I don't think I want to understand. I fold my hands and bow my head and close my eyes and say a prayer for Willy.

Tomorrow, if Gerhard and Christel and Asta are back, we can bury Willy in the forest, but I don't want Tinka and the girls to wake up and find him here like this, even as peaceful as he seems. I fold the blanket around him and lift one end to drag him out of the barn and over to the shed where we kept the others when the ground was too frozen. Willy is so wasted, so light, that I think I could carry him in my arms just as easily. What is left of him.

Once in Königsberg, a little bird flew into our windowpane and fell to the ground. I was so upset, I made Asta scoop him up and lay him in a small box. I got her to dig a hole in the courtyard garden of our apartment building, and we buried the bird there. We made a small cross and stuck it in the dirt, but it soon blew away, and in a single season, the garden grew over the little grave and we couldn't even find it any more.

I think in war, it can be like that for people, even for friends. Even for a boy like Willy. We will find a new patch of soft ground in the Memel Forest, past the fields, and bury him there. And we will find stones to cover the grave, as we did with the others. And we will chalk Willy's name onto a board or one of the rocks. But it will fade, and weather, and blow away. All of it will.

· · · · · · · · · · ·

Tinka, Ilsa, and Ada listen to me in the morning as I tell them Willy is gone. They blink and blink, as if they are expecting more. They don't seem sad, but it's not their fault. They are hungry and there's no food, and it's almost all they can think about.

For Christel, Gerhard, and Asta I know it will be different. I see them crossing the field in the late afternoon and go out to tell them. Christel, too, only looks at me for a minute, but then she turns and runs to her brother in the shed. Gerhard follows her, sobbing. Asta and I carry the bucket to the barn where Tinka and the girls and I eat in silence.

It's a bad day for the rest of the day. Christel doesn't speak to anyone. She sits with Willy in the shed until long past nightfall. Asta checks on her from time to time, brings her water she won't drink, food she won't eat.

Asta tries to talk to Gerhard, too, but he has gone from sad—from grief-stricken—to angry. He fumes and stomps around. He stares for a long time at the forest wall, as if looking at something the rest of us aren't able to see.

"If we only had had medicine to give him," he says to me and Asta. "Medicine would have helped him. It's the Red Army. They murdered him the same as if they used a gun."

Asta tries to tell Gerhard that we wouldn't know what medicine to give Willy, even if we had any. The world of doctors doesn't exist for us anymore. But he doesn't want to hear it.

"I am going," he announces, out of the blue, shouldering his rolled-up blanket and tucking the knife into his belt.

Asta tries to stop him. "Going where? We need you here."

But he is already walking away from the barn. Tinka, Ilsa, and Ada stop what they're doing—weaving more grass dolls—to watch him go.

"I'm going to find the Forest Brothers," he says. "I'm going to join them. And I will help them kill the Red Army, all of them we can find."

CHAPTER 57
ASTA

We make the hamster runs across the border as often as we can, if it's not raining, if we're not too tired, if we're not sick. Our hearts are so heavy after losing Willy, and then Gerhard. We have to stay busy. And there's no food if we don't go. It's strange. I find myself expecting both of the boys to walk back into the barn at any time, to sit next to us as usual by the fire, mad because they haven't caught a rabbit, or happy because they did. We bury Willy deep in the forest. I look for Gerhard every time I'm there, as if he might just be hiding behind a tree and will jump out to surprise us.

Most of the time it's Christel and me who cross the river in search of food. Sometimes I make Pieta come, because she needs to know where to go and how to get there. She doesn't like to leave the children. And the little ones cry any time she is away from them. We don't see Arno and Josef ever again, but there are others who hop the train. One boy doesn't make it. He loses his grip on the side of the railroad car, or his feet slip off the running board, or he's just too weak and he falls just because. We hear a splash in the river below and see the boy thrashing in the black water. But by the time we're across, jump off the slow-moving train, and run down to the river's edge, he is already gone.

Sometimes the trains don't come and we never get across at all that day. Sometimes we're stuck on the Lithuania side, once for three nights with nothing to do but wait, and beg, and hide. Thankfully, it's late spring now, or that's what we think. We don't know for certain. No one seems to know. The only thing we can be sure of is that it's no longer winter, and the problem with sleeping in the forest isn't the snow and the cold, now it's the insects and the snakes.

The villages are hit and miss. Some, like the first village our first time over, are hostile through and through. They curse at us and chase us away. The first time we see an army patrol we are surprised, though we probably shouldn't be. We thought the Red Army soldiers were only in East Prussia, but now we know they are everywhere. Even in Lithuania, patrolling the villages, maybe to keep the people in line, because so many there don't want to live under the Soviet Union and communism any more than they wanted to live under Hitler. I think of the Forest Brothers when we see the patrols, and hide. I say a prayer for Gerhard that he has found them and that he is safe.

In other villages, farther from the train line, sometimes people are kinder. Sometimes they give us work to do, small jobs, stacking firewood, beating rugs, cleaning chicken coops or rabbit hutches. They pay us with food. We are always starving and have to fight within ourselves to keep from eating it all right there, right away. Potatoes. Black bread. An egg. Cabbage. Carrots not thrown into the road. A chicken neck.

It's the same at the farmhouses. Where we're lucky enough for a handout, we're careful not to return right away to ask for more. Where they give us work, we come back until they turn us away. We're jealous of every family and every home, even the worst ones, the shacks with thatched roofs that are so leaky there is smoke rising not from the chimney but through the thatch itself. Inside, when they open the door to us, we see clouds gathered at the ceiling. These families are dirt poor, and yet more likely to share what they have with us than anyone else.

Christel always wants to visit that girl Lina's farm, even if just to watch her on her blanket in the field with the cows and calves. If no one's around, she calls out to Lina, and waves to her, and they have a pantomime conversation. I can tell Lina is happy to see me, too. She is lonely. But more and more it's Christel who is her friend.

One day, after a Red Army patrol passes, we find two boys lying in a ditch, bleeding. They have been beaten by the soldiers. We have food to bring back across the river, and we don't want to share it with them, but they beg us to help them and so we do. We have begun carrying a little water—Christel, who has become a thief like Gerhard, has stolen a leather drinking pouch—and we share that with them, too. They are not sure they can walk, they have been beaten so badly, but there is nothing more we can do. They are younger than us, I think, and they plead with us not to leave them, but we have to go. And now we have to find more food from somewhere to bring back. Even as we are standing to leave, they keep pleading. It is difficult to turn our backs on them and go.

The next time we cross over for a hamster run, Christel and I make a point of checking this place, this ditch where we find the boys, but they're no longer there.

CHAPTER 58
PIETA

I hate knocking on the doors of the farmhouses and the cottages. I hate walking down the streets of the villages even more, the way the villagers stare at us and scowl and shake their heads. The way the children sometimes throw stones at us. The way we have to duck and hide when the Red Army patrols come by. I usually hang back and let Asta or Christel be the one to stand there with a begging sack when the doors open. We take turns now, two of us going across the river, one of us staying back with the girls.

Even when I try to make myself invisible at the farms, the people still see me. But I don't look into their faces. I don't want to see their eyes and their expressions. They're annoyed that we're there. They're sad at the sight of us. They feel sorry for us. They recoil at the way we look and the way we smell. Sometimes they give us food quickly, so we'll go away. Sometimes they slam the door in our faces. Sometimes they just shake their heads sadly, and I wonder if they might not have even enough food for themselves. I look around the farms, and on some of them everything seems weedy and broken: the plow, the sagging barn, the dirty chicken coop, the pond that's more mud than water, the horse and the handful of cows that are skin and bones. Like us.

Christel takes me to the farm where a Lithuanian girl named Lina lives. Christel says she and Asta go there sometimes. I think we're going to visit the girl, and maybe be given something to eat. But we only hide in the woods and watch her do nothing out in the pasture. She lies on her back and stares up at the sky, the clouds, the trees. It's hard to say at what. She gets up and tends to the cows. But mostly they don't seem to need tending. I am bored watching her. And hungry.

After a while, Lina sits up from her blanket and waves. We must not be very well hidden. Christel steps to the edge of the pasture and waves back. I think it's an invitation, but then workers appear not far off on the farm and we melt back into the trees and leave soon after.

"Why don't we speak to her?" I say. "Ask her for food like the other farmhouses?"

"Too many people around," Christel says.

"Then why did we come?" I ask.

Christel shrugs. "I just like to see her sometimes. It makes me happy."

"She looks lonely to me," I say. "Doesn't she look lonely to you?"

Christel seems surprised by this. "She gets to go home to her farm and her family," she says. "Maybe she even has a little brother like Willy. And baby brother like Zucker. You remember Zucker?"

I'm surprised in turn. Christel hardly ever talks about them, especially not since Willy died. "Of course," I say.

Christel nods. "And Lina must go to school and church on Sunday and see her friends there."

I don't think this Lina has such a great life except for one thing: She has food to eat and she doesn't have to beg for it, and she's not starving, and she isn't wearing rags like us, and she's not so stick thin like us. And then I realize there are a thousand ways the girl has a great life, even if she's lonely. A wonderful life. A life nothing like ours. And now I'm jealous, and I want to leave. I don't want to see it anymore, and I wish Asta and Christel had never made me cross the river with them, never made me jump on that train. I would much rather stay with the children.

CHAPTER 59
ASTA

We hear gunshots one day, but far enough away from the barn that even the little ones aren't bothered. They've heard much worse. And anyway, they're busy on a task Pieta has given them, chasing rats out of the barn. They have collected a pile of stones, and they all have heavy sticks, practically logs, for bashing. Not that they ever catch or kill any of the rats. It's more of a game for them, though we've all been bitten at times, and we've all woken up to find them crawling on us and discovered them stealing any food we thought we could save for a second day.

Tinka is the one who is sick now. One of us is always sick. Sometimes more. She's been that way for a week. She eats what we bring her but can't hold it down. She has been getting weaker and there's nothing we can do. I sit with her and pretend that everything will be okay if she only drinks enough water. I don't have anything else to give her. It has been only a month since we had to bury Willy and since Gerhard left. I don't want to lose Tinka and have the sadness of Ilsa and Ada. The sadness and the grief and the responsibility. But I suppose I already have those in me, no matter what happens to Tinka.

She's asleep, and the little ones are still busy on their rat quest, when Pieta and I go into the forest to check the snares. We are all so tired from the hamster runs. They're the best way to find food, but at the same time they leave us exhausted. It's so much work getting there and getting back, and I have to wonder—we all wonder—how long we can keep doing it. The days are warmer now, and longer, but after summer is autumn, and then another winter, and how will we ever survive that?

The shooting has stopped but hearing it has me wondering what has happened in the war. The stream of children who at one time came through the farm is now only a trickle. We see them in the forest sometimes, the older ones, the ones who have managed to survive. They visit us in the night looking for things to steal, but we usually have nothing. They drink water from the pump. They move on. They make their own hamster runs. Some of them don't come back.

We are deep in the woods now and Pieta is humming one of Mama's favorite songs. I hear something and clap my hand over her mouth. It is a moaning sound, and then muttering, maybe cursing.

In German. We drop to the ground. We should crawl away, but we freeze. We are hidden inside a dense thicket of brambles and berries, and though we're afraid, food is still food. We stuff our mouths with berries and fill our pockets with as many as we can quietly grab.

There is the sound again, and again someone muttering and cursing in German. Instead of scrambling away, we press forward, the brambles catching at our ragged clothes.

We see him on the other side, leaning against a spruce tree, legs sprawled on the soft carpet of green moss. It is a teenage boy wearing what's left of a Wehrmacht uniform. Torn coat, pant legs ripped below the knees. Boots tied on with twine. One arm is out of the coat and bleeding. The boy is trying to stanch the flow of blood with strips he tears off his clothes, but it's too difficult with just one hand. Pieta, who always wants to help—who acts without thinking—steps out of the thicket before I can stop her. The soldier drops his rags and grabs a gun from his belt holster. It is a pistol and he points it at Pieta.

Thankfully, he doesn't shoot. "A child!" he says, as if he can't believe what he has nearly done. He drops the gun and covers his face with his one good hand. I have never seen a soldier cry before, even one so young.

Pieta and I sit on the soft ground next to him and offer him water. She holds up the stolen pouch so he can drink while I tie the tourniquet as tightly as I can to stop the bleeding from the wound on his arm. He has been shot. I think by how pale he is that he has lost a great deal of blood. He thanks us and keeps drinking. He doesn't stop until the water pouch is empty. He asks for more, but Pieta can only squeeze it to show him there is none.

He nods. "Danke," he says. His lips are still dry and cracked. His face is smeared with dirt and blood. He is wheezing. "Danke Schoen."

He tells us he has been running from the Red Army patrols. He had been in Königsberg during the siege and when the Wehrmacht finally had to surrender. That was months ago. He has been a prisoner ever since. There are thousands of prisoners being sent off on trains. He doesn't know where. Hundreds, maybe thousands, have perished in the prison camps.

He escaped two weeks ago, he tells us. Him and his friends. But they were separated. He had managed to wrestle a pistol from one of the guards. The Red Army hunted them. He doesn't think his friends survived.

He speaks in short sentences because he is having so much difficulty breathing. Pieta offers him berries, but he only stares at them. Surely he is hungry. Even starving. There is so little flesh on his face, even in his hands.

"And they shot at you?" I ask, though it's obvious they did.

He looks at his arm. Even lifting it a little makes him wince with pain. "Just this morning," he says. "I was careless. I let myself be seen. But I don't think they followed me here. I hope they didn't. You heard the shooting from earlier?"

I nod and look around as if I might see someone. But there is only Pieta, still holding her berries. She offers them again and he takes one, I think more to be polite than anything.

"And what about the war?" I ask.

He looks surprised. "The war is over. Stunde Null—zero hour—was all the way back in May. So I think one month already. The Red Army took East Prussia and Poland, then Berlin. The Americans took all of France and much of Germany."

I am too stunned to speak, so it is Pieta who asks the next question.

"And Hitler? What has become of him?"

The soldier shakes his head. "Dead since April."

CHAPTER 60
PIETA

I am tugging at Asta's coat to get her to leave. If they were hunting this young soldier, then they may still be searching for him, even here in the forest. Maybe we can bring him more water later, if they don't find him first. I whisper this to Asta, but she is more interested in finding out what has happened in the war, and in East Prussia since the Red Army came and Königsberg fell. I only wanted to know about Hitler. Without Hitler, I think maybe the world can go back to the way Mama said it was when she was a girl, before we were even born.

"Please, Asta," I beg her. And now the soldier agrees with me.

"You must go," he says. "It's not safe."

But just as he says it, we hear a crashing through the woods, and shouting. Soviets. Birds fly out of the trees. I make fists and crush the berries I'm still holding. The dark juice drips down on my trousers like my own blood. The soldier lifts his gun, and Asta and I crawl away back through the thicket as the crashing comes closer.

We tumble down a hill, running and falling and picking ourselves up and running again. Gunshots tear through the forest, behind us, echoing everywhere, echoing in my head.

Now we're running so fast and so hard that we can hardly see and collide with men who suddenly emerge from the brush and are standing right in front of us, their guns drawn as well. They shove us to the ground but we're falling, anyway. I grab Asta and hold her and she holds me, too. A man with a beard and a deep jagged scar down the side of his face is barking at us, saying something I don't understand. Lithuanian. He changes his language, and now he's speaking German. A child's German. I can hardly follow what he's saying, but that's because all the crashing and all the gunshots are still rattling in my head. Asta does better. She answers in German. She points behind us, in the direction of the soldier we've just abandoned. She says "Red Army" and "Wehrmacht soldier" and "gun."

And then—I can't believe it!—from behind the man steps Gerhard! Asta jumps to her feet and tries to hug him, but he stops her. "There's no time," he says. "How far to the soldier?"

The shooting continues behind us, which should already tell him everything they need to know. But Asta says, "Five minutes away. No more than that. They're going to kill him. A German boy. He's already been shot."

Gerhard nods. The other Forest Brothers have moved on. Gerhard is carrying a backpack that must be filled with supplies, ammunition, who can say? He isn't carrying a gun, but his knife is still tucked into his belt.

"Hide!" he yells to us as he turns to follow the men. "I'll try to find you."

We stand frozen and alone for a few minutes, attempting to catch our breath, still stunned by the surprise of running into the Forest Brothers—and Gerhard!

Dozens of guns are shooting now, and it's as if the entire forest isn't just echoing with the noise, but exploding with it, exploding all around us. The shooting goes on and on and on. Asta pulls me to my feet and we're running once again. I don't know how she's able to find her way in the forest so well, but she does—to our secret hiding place, the one we found when we first came to Gerhard's farm, the small cave. Like Mama's secret hiding place in the Romincka Forest, which saved us then like we hope ours will save us now.

We crawl inside, hardly enough room for us to lie next to each other. Asta drags branches behind us to cover the opening and we lie as still as we can until the shooting stops, and even then we don't come out. Not for the rest of the day, and not through the long night when the woods outside our rock shelter come alive with forest creatures darting and whirring and snuffling and squawking and hooting and crashing and crying.

Or it might be me crying. And Asta, as always, comforting me, whispering that everything will be all right, everything will be all right.

"But what about Christel and Tinka and the others?" I ask her.

"They know to hide as well," she answers. "That is why we practiced so much." And it's true. We built a small lean-to not far from the barn in the forest and camouflaged it with branches and stones. For just in case.

"I worry that Tinka might be too sick," I say.

"It's not very far," Asta says. "And Christel is strong. Tinka can lean on her. And Isla and Ada can help, too. They'll be okay."

"And we'll find them?" I ask.

"Of course we will," Asta says. "We haven't been through everything only to lose them now. And besides, the Red Army isn't looking for us. They were looking for the German soldier, that boy. And the Forest Brothers."

I hope they don't hurt Gerhard. I know Asta is growing tired of reassuring me about everything, but she promises Gerhard will survive this, too. "And we'll get to see him again, remember? He said he would find us."

We are silent after that. And eventually, with the quiet sounds of the night forest as our lullaby, we sleep.

···········

Late the next afternoon, Asta says it should be safe for us to crawl out of our hiding place. Quickly we make our way through the forest in the direction of the barn.

But the path takes us past the young soldier.

The bush with the berries has been shredded by all the bullets that were fired. There is blood everywhere, but only one body. Maybe everyone else survived—the Red Army soldiers and the Forest Brothers. Or maybe they buried their own dead in their own special places. Asta presses her hand to the German soldier's chest to see if he might still be breathing. I pray that he isn't. He would only be suffering if so. She goes through his pockets. In the lining of his coat is a picture of a family. She shows it to me. A mother and a father and a sister and a brother. His face is so much older now. We leave the photograph with him. Asta says there's nothing we can use except his belt. That is the only thing we take. We have no way to bury him, and no time. We have to get back to the barn to check on the others.

CHAPTER 61
ASTA

Gerhard's barn has now been burned all the way to the ground. It is still smoldering when we get there. Tinka and Ilsa and Ada are gone. Christel, too. Even the pump has been destroyed. There's nothing left but cinders. Pieta sits on the ground and hugs her knees and bows her head. It is all too much for her, I think. The shooting. The young soldier killed. The hiding. Seeing Gerhard and then losing him again. Now this.

"They must have heard the shooting and ran away before the soldiers came," I tell her, trying to sound hopeful. Pieta doesn't respond. I sift through the ruins with a long stick, looking for bones. I don't find any but can only reach so far in the rubble and the dying embers. I give up and toss the stick in, too.

"There's no water anymore," I say. It's as if I'm speaking to myself, speaking to this barren world of nothing. We're both thirsty. We've had nothing to drink since yesterday, and suddenly, knowing there's no longer any water here, I'm desperate to drink.

But we have to look for Christel and the girls first. "Do you want to wait here?" I ask Pieta, who has shut down. "I'll look for them at the lean-to. That's where they should have gone. I don't think they've been back here. There's no sign. No message left for us in the dirt."

But Pieta doesn't want me to leave her. She struggles to her feet. I grab another stick and write a message of our own—for Christel, and for Gerhard, who said he would find us, though I can't imagine the Forest Brothers will let him go off by himself now that he has joined them.

It's not far to the lean-to. We built it as hidden as we could between large rocks at the edge of the fields, just inside the forest where it's thick with brush and heavy trees. But there's no Christel, no Tinka or Ilsa or Ada. They could be anywhere. Somewhere else in the forest. Taken by the Red Army soldiers. Killed.

But there are no bodies, and there is no trace of them anywhere we can find. At a small stream, hardly even a stream, we lie on the forest floor and drink as much as we can hold. It will have to do for now instead of food. We pause before stepping out of the shadows and out into the open field. Even the shed is gone now. It is as if whoever burned it—a half-fallen barn, a small outbuilding, the pump—wanted to wipe all traces of Gerhard's aunt and uncle's farm off the face of the earth. Maybe that is what they're doing to all of

East Prussia. Killing every German who is left. Taking the children. Destroying everyone and everything.

· · · · · · · · · · ·

We return to the lean-to, which is the only cover we have. Once again there's no way to build a fire. We don't have Gerhard's flint and steel knife. We no longer have the lighter, and it ran dry a long time ago, anyway. Though it's June, it still gets chilly at night, and once again Pieta and I have only each other to hold on to for warmth.

The first day we wait, there is nothing. And the second. And the third. We eat bark. Insects. Pieta catches a frog, but it makes us both sick. We journey again and again to the little stream. There's no point checking the old snares for rabbits. We have no way to skin them. No way to cook the meat. There are more berries. Clovers. Green shoots and leaves.

On the third day, Pieta says she thinks we should leave.

"And go where?" I ask her. "You mean to make a hamster run across the river? One of us could, but one of us should stay here, in case Christel and the girls find their way back."

"But what if they don't come back?" Pieta asks. "It has already been so long."

"We told them we would wait," I remind her. "And they told us they would wait if we were the ones missing. It is all we can do. We can't abandon them."

"I know. I know," Pieta says. "But what if they have abandoned us? Or what if they have been taken?"

I throw up my hands in exasperation. "The same questions over and over!" I snap. "How can I know? How any anyone know? We can only do what we said we would do."

Pieta is silent for a while. I think I have hurt her feelings.

"Anyway," I say, "where do you think we should go? To Lithuania?"

But she shakes her head. "No. To Hamburg."

I almost laugh, it is so absurd, the idea of going to Hamburg. "It's fifteen hundred kilometers away," I say. "You know this from school the same as me. Fifteen hundred kilometers. And there's no train. No car. No ships anymore. We would have to go across all of East Prussia, then all of Poland to get there."

"I know," Pieta says quietly. "But it is the only place we have a family anymore."

"Gerhard is our family," I tell her. "And Christel. And Tinka and the little girls."

"But now they are gone," she says.

"Maybe," I remind her. "We're still waiting to find out."

• • • • • • • • • •

As it turns out, we don't have to wait much longer. For Gerhard, anyway. When I wake up early the next morning, shivering in the lean-to, I crawl out and see him standing alone by the remains of the barn. A thick fog has settled over the farm, and he's only a dim figure, but I still know it's him. I would recognize Gerhard anywhere.

I leave Pieta sleeping and wade through the fog. I say Gerhard's name before I reach him because I don't want to startle him. But even as I'm saying it, he's turning to look at me. We hug and then we're both talking at once, him telling me about his time with the Forest Brothers, me telling him about Christel and the others and how worried we are. He says the Red Army has been rounding up children in the Memel Forest. He has seen them crammed into the backs of trucks and farm wagons.

"We think they are putting them on trains," he says. "To Siberia and places like that."

"Prisoners?" I ask him. "But why?"

He shakes his head. "Workers. Laborers. Factories. Farms. That's what the Forest Brothers tell me. Or that's what I think they're saying. They only know a little German, and I am just trying to learn Lithuanian."

"Did you see them here?" I ask. "The trucks? Did they take Christel? The others?"

But he doesn't know. "They are also setting fires in the forest," he says. "That is the greater danger. If the Forest Brothers have nowhere to hide anymore, they can be easily captured by the Red Army. Captured and executed. And the children hiding there, they will have nowhere, either."

We sit on the ground, deflated. Gerhard has a blanket, and he drapes it over my shoulders. I make room so I can share it with him. I should bring it to the lean-to for Pieta. But maybe in a few minutes, after we talk. I don't know how long Gerhard will stay.

As if he's reading my mind, he tells me. "I can't be gone long," he says. "The Forest Brothers trust no one, and I had to beg them to let me come here. I told them I had promised to find you. I think they feel sorry for us."

"For us?" I ask.

"All of the East Prussian children."

CHAPTER 62
PIETA

When I wake up on the hard ground inside the lean-to, it takes me a few minutes to realize I'm under a blanket. I'm tangled up in it, as if I've been thrashing around in one of my dreams. I dream of Königsberg often, and Mama, and home. The bombing. The shelter that saved us because I refused to leave. That was so long ago. Why am I still dreaming about that when so much else has happened since then? When Königsberg isn't even Königsberg anymore.

I sit up and rub my eyes and cough. I have had this cough for weeks, but I mostly don't think about it because there are too many other things—taking care of Tinka, looking after the little ones, searching, searching, searching, always searching for food. Only now, they're gone, too. And Christel . . .

Two figures duck inside the lean-to, and I can't believe it. Gerhard again! And he is with Asta.

"Surprise!" he says.

I hug him fiercely. "You said you would come," I say. "And you did."

"And I brought things," he says. He hands me a canteen and I drink greedily. Some splashes down my chin. I soak it up with my sleeve and then suck on the sleeve.

He hands me a small crust of black bread and a sliver of hard sausage called Landjäger. I eat the bread right away and tuck the meat inside my cheek to savor the smoky flavor and let it soften until I can chew.

"It's venison," Gerhard says, not that I want to know. "From the Forest Brothers."

I realize I'm the only one with a blanket, and I offer it to them, but Gerhard waves me off. "You and Asta can have it to keep. And I have something else for you, too."

He draws out his knife and hands it to Asta, then digs in his pocket for his flint and gives her that as well.

"You'll need these," he says. "I want you to have them."

I don't know what to say. Neither does Asta. "But aren't you going to stay with us?" I ask. "Help us find Christel and the others?"

Gerhard shakes his head. He seems so much older, even though he's only been gone from us for a few weeks.

Asta lets it go. She asks him if the Forest Brothers will mind him giving us the knife and blanket.

"Probably," he says. "They were not happy that I left at all, but I had to see you. To make sure you are okay."

"Was anyone hurt in the shooting?" I ask. "Besides the German boy. We saw him."

Gerhard nods. "Two of ours. And I think more of theirs. It's hard to know. But here." He changes the subject and hands me the canteen again. "You should keep this, too. And if I can find anything else you'll need, I'll leave it here for you. But I have to go now. Our company is breaking camp today. We can never stay in one place for very long. The Red Army will find us. And we have to stay ahead of the fires."

He stands to leave, but I can't help myself. I grab his pant leg and hold him back. "Stay with us," I say again. "Please."

He bends down and pats my hand. It's Asta who pries my fingers loose so he can go.

· · · · · · · · · · ·

Something wakes me in the night. Headlights across the fields on the rutted dirt road that leads to the farm. The truck moves slowly, as if trying to sneak up on someone, though once I'm aware of the headlights, I can hear it, faintly at first, then growing louder as it approaches.

Shapes emerge from the back of the truck. Flashlight beams fan out across the field, like fireflies. There are muted voices. They draw closer, past the foundations of the barn and the farmhouse, toward the edge of the forest. Toward where we are hiding. I shake Asta and she sits up, too, and sees. I am frightened that they will find us. We should never have built the lean-to so near to the farm. But how else would Gerhard—and the others if they ever come—have been able to find us?

I hold my breath, not daring to make a sound. The lights sweep past. The men search the edge of the woods the length of the fields, then return to the truck. The engine cranks back to life. The gears grind. The headlights come back on. The truck turns around slowly and vanishes back up the access road.

In the morning, knowing it's not safe here any longer, we make our way through the woods to the train and escape across the Memel River.

CHAPTER 63
ASTA

For two days and two nights, we are caught in a rainstorm. We've made our way to the woods near Lina's farm, hoping she'll give us food, but when we get there the skies open and we're forced to huddle under Gerhard's blanket, hoping for enough shelter from the overhanging trees to keep us dry. But the trees are soon waterlogged and dripping on the blanket until it's so soaked that we might as well be standing out in the rain. A stream forms at our feet, and we drink from it to keep our stomachs full. We've had nothing to eat since Gerhard's black bread crusts and hard sausages.

On the third day, the rain lets up and the sun comes out and we spread our blanket to dry at least a little on the soggy forest floor. Narrow threads of sunlight filter through the canopy and the air is steamy. We are trying to decide how best to approach Lina when we hear a rustling in the undergrowth and a calf pokes its face out of the bushes.

"Well, hello!" Pieta laughs, as if she's been waiting for the visitor. "Have you escaped from the farm?"

She rubs the calf's long nose and lets it lick her salty face. The calf doesn't answer.

• • • • • • • • • •

It takes a long time to coax the calf back to Lina's farm. We don't have a rope, and Pieta and I have to walk on either side, keeping a firm grip with our arms thrown over the calf's neck to keep it from running off again. We stop when we finally reach the fence where the forest opens up onto a meadow dotted with lazy cows eating their lazy grass, chewing their lazy cud. There is a girl on a blanket where Lina usually sits under the shade of the one lone tree. But this girl doesn't look like Lina. It takes me a moment, staring hard, to realize—

It's not Lina at all. It's Christel!

I shout her name and throw myself over the fence. She hears me and runs, everything scattering in her wake. We meet halfway across the field and fling ourselves on top of one another, falling to the ground, laughing and shouting nonsense in our shared happiness.

"I thought we'd lost you!" I manage to say. "But you're all right!"

"I thought I'd lost you, too!" Christel says. "I was so worried." And then she bursts into tears.

"I'm so sorry," she says. "I'm so sorry. I'm so sorry." She keeps apologizing, though I don't know why, and soon sobbing so hard she's shaking. I hold her and let her cry.

"I left them," Christel says in a shuddering voice. "I didn't mean to. They were so frightened, but they wouldn't follow me. I had to run. I had to leave them. I didn't know what else to do."

She wipes her face on her sleeve. "They caught us at the barn, then they set it on fire. We heard guns shooting in the forest and we didn't know where you were. They put us in the back of a truck with other children and drove us away without telling us where we were going. We made it only a little ways before there was a problem with the engine. No one was watching us when they stopped. I climbed down and told Tinka and the girls to come with me. But they were too afraid. I was begging them, but there wasn't enough time. Two soldiers came back to check on us and I had to run."

I try to reassure Christel. I tell her she did the best she could, but she shakes her head.

"I'm so sorry," she says again. She can't stop saying it.

I point back to the edge of the field where Pieta is still waiting with the escaped calf. "We should help Pieta get him through the fence," I say, interrupting Christel's apologies. She dries her eyes on an old apron I hadn't realized she was wearing. All the clothes she has on look like hand-me-downs. Worn but clean.

"If I lose a calf, they might not let me stay," she says.

"Lina's family?" I ask, and she nods as we cross the field to Pieta.

"I didn't know where else to go," Christel says. "And Lina was happy to see me. I think she is lonely in the fields. She shared her food with me, and even gave me a blanket from the farmhouse and brought me some old clothes. She tried to bring extra food, but she couldn't always. Sometimes there were workers around, or her family. I hid in the woods. I wanted to go back, to see if I could find you and Pieta. But then they found me—her father and one of his workers."

She tells us the rest after we wrestle the calf back through the fence.

"They found me in the forest," she says. "They must have suspected that Lina was taking extra food, and blankets, and made her tell them where I was hiding. They brought me back to the farmhouse. Lina's mother ladled out a bowl of soup and placed it on the table in front of me. It was so good! Her little brother grabbed the bowl before I could bring it to my face and lick it clean, and her mother filled it again. She pulled a fresh loaf of black bread from a wooden box on the counter and cut off a thick slice that Lina slathered with butter."

Pieta's stomach rumbles. Mine does, too.

Christel says that after an hour, Lina's father arrived with an elderly farmer who shuffled into the farmhouse and sat across from her at the table.

"From East Prussia?" he asked her in broken German.

Christel nodded.

"Your family is where?"

She shook her head.

"So," he said. "Orphan."

She nodded.

"Is good you come," he said. "This girl." He indicated Lina. "Goes to school. Soon. You stay here with this Lithuanian family. Watch cows. Milk cows. Do work."

Little by little, in his halting way, he told Christel that Lina's family was willing to take her in to live with them, give her food to eat, clothes to wear. Lina's mother showed her a bench in a tiny alcove under the stairs where she would sleep. While Lina went to school, Christel would tend to the cows and do other chores around the farm, and do the milking mornings and evenings.

Christel tells us all this in a rush, all the while looking anxiously back at the farmhouse to make sure no one is coming.

"Lina is teaching me Lithuanian," she says, and tells us some of the words.

Cow. Field. Farm. Hand. Face. Hair. Milk. Bread. Egg.

Karvė. Lauke. Ūkis. Ranka. Veidas. Plaukai. Pieno. Duona. Kiaušinis.

"It's forbidden to speak German here," Christel explains. "I think it must be forbidden to speak German anywhere anymore."

CHAPTER 64
PIETA

On this side of the river is Lithuania. On the other side is no longer East Prussia. The whole world has been changed, I think. All the countries have been turned upside down. Lina's neighbor, the old man, told Christel that the Soviets have begun sending peasant families to Königsberg and the villages and the farms like Opa and Oma's. No Germans are allowed there anymore. The old man said if Christel stays with Lina's family, she can no longer be German, not even her name. They will give her a new one. They have even picked it out already: Kamile. They will teach Christel a new language. Her past will be erased.

But she will have food. And shelter. And a family again.

So we leave her. There are tears, and we are heartbroken and sad. We say goodbye to Christel, and then we correct ourselves and say goodbye to Kamile.

Once we are back in the safety of the forest, rolling up our still-wet blanket, I ask Asta if she thinks there could be a farm for us as well. She says she doesn't know.

"This is the only one so far," she says. "Some feel sorry for us and share their food. But no one else has invited us to stay. No one else wants us. And even if they did, they wouldn't take two of us."

We should be happy for Christel, that she has found a home and a family and food and work. Better to have a life, any life, than this one we've been living, this life where children have to survive on our own. Where we starve, and fall ill, and miss our families.

It feels too dark and damp here. Too claustrophobic. Too close to Christel's new home, where they already have one East Prussian girl and no room for any others. We gather our things, which aren't much: the blanket, Gerhard's knife, the canteen, Asta's begging sack, the clothes we have on and the coats we now carry. A few last bites of Christel's food.

An hour later, west on the bank of the Memel River, we sit side by side on a fallen log, two sisters alone in the world. A freight train sounds its whistle a few miles away, probably crossing the bridge into East Prussia.

"Do you still want to go to Hamburg?" Asta asks me. "To find Mama's cousin?"

I look at her in surprise. "But you said it's fifteen hundred kilometers away. We would have to find our way past the Red Army.

Then through all of Poland. You said it was too far and too dangerous."

"I think it's too dangerous to stay," she says. "They're burning down the forests now. They're burning down everything. There's nothing for us here any longer. If we stay, we might be captured and sent away like Tinka and Ilsa and Ada. Or we could get sick and there would be no one to help us. And in a few months, it will be another winter."

We swing our legs for awhile, like little girls, staring at the water below. The Memel is running clear for the first time in a long time. We chew slowly on the last shreds of food from Christel, softening the hard bread and strips of meat with sips from Gerhard's canteen. Asta pulls out the knife and carves our initials in the soft wood of the rotting log.

"Now they'll always know we were here," she says.

I want to say something clever, or funny, or sweet. Instead, I say what we both are thinking.

"We could separate. Someone might take us in if there is only one of us, like Christel."

Asta puts her arm around me. "I could never do that," she says, quick to respond. "I wouldn't know how not to be your sister."

I lean my head against her shoulder, relieved and grateful, and whisper back, "I wouldn't know how not to be your sister, either."

We sit there together for a long time, until Asta breaks the silence.

"The journey of a thousand miles begins with a single step," she says. "Have you heard this before?"

I nod and she stands, gathering our things.

The train whistle blows again at the railroad bridge as we make our way back to the road.

"To Hamburg, then," Asta says, and we begin our journey, holding hands.

HISTORICAL NOTE

During the last days of World War II, in the harsh winter of 1944–45, more than 2 million people desperately fled the northeastern German province of East Prussia, just weeks ahead of the Soviet Red Army invasion. The citizens had been forbidden by Hitler to leave their vulnerable homes until it was almost too late. Hitler's army, the Wehrmacht, by then in full retreat, had brutalized the Soviet Union's population through years of scorched-earth war, and the advancing Red Army had vowed to exact its revenge. As the Soviets marched across the land, destroying everything in their path, the Allies rained bombs from above. Starting in January 1945, they began the Battle of Königsberg, a bombing campaign on the East Prussian capital. Together, Allied bombers and the Red Army killed tens of thousands of German soldiers and civilians. By the end of the siege, in early April 1945, 80 percent of Königsberg had been destroyed.

At first, the fleeing East Prussians were able to escape to Mainland Germany by traveling overland through Poland, but after the land routes were severed, the only way out was on overcrowded passenger ships on the icy Baltic Sea. Known as Operation Hannibal, it was a last-ditch attempt of the Wehrmacht to evacuate various German territories from the advancing Red Army. However, tens of thousands civilians perished on dozens of these vessels sunk by Red Army submarines. The worst maritime disaster in history was the January 30, 1945, sinking of the *Wilhelm Gustloff*, a cruise ship intended to hold 1,900 but was carrying more than 10,000 during the evacuation. The *Wilhelm Gustloff* was struck by three Soviet torpedoes not long after leaving the harbor. It took over an hour for the ship to sink into the icy waters, and while there were enough lifeboats for 5,000 people, most of them were frozen to the deck and couldn't be used. An estimated 9,400 of those on board were killed—three times more than perished in the sinking of the *Titanic* and *Lusitania* combined.

In the confusion and terror of the mass evacuation and the Red Army assault, as many as 20,000 East Prussian children were separated from their parents—lost, orphaned, or abandoned. Many starved or died from exposure. Others were shot by Red Army soldiers. Most who survived, an estimated 5,000 children, banded together in small groups, fending for themselves for months, sometimes years, in forests and on abandoned farms in East Prussia and across the Memel River in neighboring Lithuania—begging, stealing, sleeping in the open, even in the dead of winter, eating whatever they could find or scavenge. These children, some as young as four and five, became known as Wolfskinder—wolf children—and over time their story, their very existence, has been all but erased, much like the children left orphaned and homeless by armed conflicts around the world today. They, too, are victims of war.

Most of the surviving Wolfskinder were forced to give up their identities after the war when they were caught and sent to live in the Soviet Union, or "adopted" by Lithuanian families for their free labor, or loaded onto cattle cars and shipped to communist East Germany where they were raised in orphanages and forbidden to talk about their past. A few, like the fictional Asta and Pieta in *Wolves at the Door*, made their way—or tried, at great cost and sacrifice—to what would eventually become democratic West Germany in the desperate hope of finding freedom and family and a place to call home.

In recent years, a few historians have turned their attention to the last days of East Prussia—which since the war has been a part of Russia called the Kaliningrad Oblast and been largely forgotten by history—and to discovering the fate of the wolf children who lived through those terrible postwar years. Dozens of the Wolfskinder are still alive today, tracked down through painstaking research by writers like Sonya Winterberg and convinced to share their stories with a world that had long since forgotten them. *The Wolf Children of the Eastern Front: Alone and Forgotten,* written by Sonya Winterberg and Kerstin Lieff, was an invaluable reference work for the writing of *Wolves at the Door* and is essential reading for anyone who wants to learn more about these invisible victims of war.

ACKNOWLEDGEMENTS

[TK]

ABOUT THE AUTHOR

Steve Watkins is the author of *Sink or Swim*; the Ghosts of War series, including *The Secret of Midway*, *Lost at Khe Sanh*, *AWOL in North Africa*, and *Fallen in Fredericksburg*; and *Down Sand Mountain*, as well as many young adult novels.

A former professor of journalism, creative writing, and Vietnam War literature, Steve is the cofounder and editor of Pie & Chai, a monthly magazine that you can find and read online at pieandchaimagazine.com.